MARESSA MORTIMER

Viking Ferry

~But if you don't forgive men their trespasses, neither will your Father forgive your trespasses. ~

MATTHEW 6 : 15

Chapter 1

"...was blind, but now I'm fou-hou-hou-hound, see, rather," Marieke harmonises, not too harmoniously. After all, it's nearly an hour past midnight, and the M20 is dreadfully boring. It's not overly exciting at other times either, but at least in the day time one can keep a look out for the first glimpse of the sea, or look at the wonderful White Cliffs.

Her little red Fiat Panda rattles along cheerfully, the lack of top-notch suspension helpful in the joined effort of keeping Marieke awake and alert. The half-open window lets in cold air and enough noise to drown out the cd player. However, the hymn cd can still be heard, thanks to Marieke's singing along, pretending to be the harmonising soloist. She will never be a career soloist or even an amateur one, but driving along by herself at night gives her a great opportunity to sing as loudly as she wants without being sued for hearing loss.

Marieke flexes her fingers, cramped from gripping the thin steering wheel. Her wrists ache from rattling along for so long, and she yawns. Coffee would be nice, and there is a services somewhere along here. She peers at a road sign coming up, worried that somehow she has gotten it wrong, and the reason this motorway seems endless is that she is on the wrong one, on her way to Edinburgh or something. She sings more jubilantly when she sees the little ferry sign along with Dover and Folkestone. This is definitely the right route. Marieke leans back into the hard seat, tries to roll her shoulders to ease the stiffness, and keeps staring ahead, hoping to see the lights of Dover. She looks at the clock on her dashboard and writes off that cup of coffee. Time to get to the ferry, and fast, as it's later than she hoped.

Marieke swallows, her wailing along with the cd noticeably subdued. She winds her window up, mentally calling it her workout for the night. Never easy to turn the handle, her 'aerobic window control' is harder to wind than ever, as her wrist disagrees with the extra abuse. She just needs it quiet in the car, as quiet as it gets in a speeding Panda. When the lights of Dover finally appear the soft singing is reduced to a tuneless humming. This is the bit Marieke has not been looking forward to.

Marieke tries to smile a little at the French border guard who doesn't seem to notice, and who's obviously not having a great time either. They look at her Dutch passport, then back at her several times, making her feel nervous. The British lady is more amiable, asking questions in a conversational tone. She is relieved when both those hurdles have been taken. Marieke is glad there is no car behind her, for she wants to go as slowly as possible without stalling her red tin box. "Left lane here, no other left, up there is for lorries..." Her voice trails off as she hangs her head as far over her steering wheel as possible, frantically reading all the little signs and notices. The bit that has her heart beating wildly is the ramp onto the ferry itself. She can just imagine her Panda stalling and rolling backwards into a metal game of falling dominoes. Making it to the top doesn't bring much relief, as now she will have to park exactly where the man in a yellow safety coat tells her to. Driving over his toes will not be appreciated, so Marieke concentrates all her efforts on staying on the straight and narrow, the tiny lane indicated by a bored but efficient man.

She sighs with relief whilst fishing her large handbag from the car. Coffee, sleep, more coffee, and the rest of the drive home. She smiled a little, imagining the surprise on her mum's face when ringing the doorbell in the morning! She pulls her coat around herself a bit tighter, and stumbles up the steep stairs, then makes a beeline for the huge window at the front of the ferry. The restaurant is open, and she pours herself a coffee. The man at the till seems in a good mood. "Not too busy tonight," Marieke observes, and the man agrees. He explains that it's usually like this at night.

"You do get the lorry drivers of course, but they tend to go upstairs. And a few other people, usually younger, so it can still get very noisy," he smiles back. Marieke wishes him a pleasant crossing and takes her coffee to the table nearest the floor to ceiling window.

She sits down staring out over the black smooth water of the harbour. Beyond the harbour wall, the waves seem to have tiny little white heads, making her feel drowsy. There are a lot of lorry drivers upstairs, some leaning on the railings, and she feels a bit 'watched'. Marieke hesitates, she really wants to have a nap, and finally decides to sleep on the little window ledge. That way she can look at the sea, and just let her thoughts float off. The long benches and tables hide her from view as well, which gives her a more secure feeling. It's not very busy, but there are still more people milling about now, getting food from the restaurant. She knows if she sleeps on one of the seats, she would be people watching most of the time, and she needs her beauty sleep.

The ledge feels chilly, but her coat is warm, and with her head propped up on her handbag Marieke tries to get comfortable. She has two hours before they dock, which should leave her feeling refreshed. The voices from the other passengers are a quiet mumbling. Occasionally there is a clattering noise from the kitchen, and soon she can tell from the boat's movement that they have left the harbour behind. Marieke closes her eyes and drifts off.

Chapter 2

Slowly life starts to filter through again. Marieke isn't about to open her eyes, but she's definitely no longer asleep. The ferry is very quiet, not even the sounds of clattering crockery can be heard. Mind you, the boat doesn't feel like it's moving anymore, so surely that has reduced the risk of collapsing stacks of cups and plates. Nothing else can be heard, and Marieke lies still, enjoying the peace, glad that she is feeling so refreshed. Slowly it sinks in that it really is very quiet on the ferry. Marieke opens her eyes, suddenly worried that she is feeling very rested, maybe too rested? The ferry is no longer moving, has she completely missed the call for all drivers to return to their vehicles? Is that why it is completely silent? Everyone has left, and they're getting ready to receive the next wave of passengers ready to return to Dover?

Marieke sits up, frantically looking round, wondering what to do. It is dark outside, which makes her feel better. At least she hasn't slept for hours and hours, and the harbour they're in isn't Dover again. Marieke looks around slowly and listens. Should she get up and walk to the stairs down to the car deck? Just when she has slipped off her feet, ready to investigate, she can hear voices. Men's voices, rather raucous. She quickly lowers herself down again, glad of the protection the bench gives her. She peeks out, and before long the group comes in sight. Her first reaction is 'stag do', as the all-male group comes round the corner. The longish blond hair is definitely fake, and they're slightly beyond tipsy, Marieke decides.

She lowers herself even more but keeps staring at the odd group. Their voices are loud and harsh, guttural sounds interspersed with laughter. Dutch, she decides. Dutch or German, trying to speak fake English. Or maybe English trying to speak fake German, although she'd have thought they'd be more drunk, and there would be more singing and more arms-around-shoulder type things going on. Marieke is starting to smile, wondering what poor groom has to pay for a stag party on this scale, and how is the French border police going to react to a group like this? They've definitely gone for quality, she thinks, looking at their costumes. Most of them have a moustache, most have a long-haired wig, one has a small round helmet, and they all carry swords. The clothes are well done too, the typical Viking tunics, including knee-high boots, leather criss-cross straps and all. They've gone to great lengths for this party. She wonders how comfy those boots are, and are they warm? Her own leather boots are comfortable, but at the end of a long winter, they're now starting to show signs of wear. Mind you, she has had them for a couple of years now, so maybe something like those strappy boots would work?

Looking closer at the guys she suddenly feels sure that the moustaches are real. Some of the hair must be real too, not the yellowish wigs ones, but the slightly darker blond ones must have their own hair, she's sure. They're all quite young, not too tall but stocky. Typical gym rats. The long hair doesn't seem to go with that though, as it makes lifting weights tricky, and working up a sweat is gross with long hair. Maybe builders then, the bricklaying, lifting kinds of builders? Although a safety helmet and long hair isn't the best combination either.

Again Marieke wonders what has happened to the other passengers or even the staff from the restaurant. She decides to investigate as soon as the party-goers have gone. She doesn't want rude comments from a group of tipsy guys. One of them turns his face towards the large windows, and Marieke realises that she has been staring at the group, so she shrinks down even lower. Whether it was the movement reflected in the glass, or something showing like her boots, she doesn't know, but the group stops moving as the man barks out something loud. The entire party stops moving, and Marieke doesn't dare to look, but she can hear some of them coming towards the window. She can see their reflection moving in the glass. She is holding her breath, although she isn't sure why, and makes herself sit up more. Why should she be hiding? After all, she has a ticket for this boat, not that these guys are anything to do with that of course, but she has as much right to be here as they have.

Maybe even more, because Marieke is sure there is something in the T&C's about drinking on board and being a nuisance. She hasn't long to weigh up who is more deserving to be on board the ferry, as three of the guys come in view towering over her. The largest one, with clearly fake yellow hair and an impressive droopy moustache, growls something at her, his face hard. Marieke blinks and then says in her poshest English voice, "I have no idea what you're saying. Having a stag do or whatever other party it is, doesn't mean you can harass fellow passengers." Her Dutch accent is still there of course, but she is quite sure they're English, but if not, they might answer her in Dutch. The three men stare at her, and the same guy who spoke before frowns a little, his mouth turning even more grim. He repeats what sounds exactly like he said before, but more impatient. The other two move forward that little bit, making her feel intimidated and annoyed at the same time.

"Some space please," she says in as catty a voice she can, with only the slightest tremor in her voice. She really can't stand confrontations, and these guys are now getting annoying, giving off nasty vibes. Having a loud party on a ferry is inconsiderate enough, but to hassle people as well is taking fun too far. She regrets sitting down, hating the way the men tower over her, but there isn't enough space for her to stand up. The first guy now really crowds her space, growling something at her, and motioning with his hand for her to get up. Kidding, right? He really thinks she is going to get up and come along with their stag do? She glares at him, and decides to forget the posh English lady role, and just go with the insulted Dutch mama voice instead. "Kappen nou," she says crossly, "Hoepel open en laat me met rust. Hou je feestje ergens anders." (Stop it. Go away, leave me alone and party somewhere else). That should do it, as they're obviously pretending the whole Viking accent thing, and even if they're German they'll get this, especially as her facial expression should mean the same thing in any language and culture.

It doesn't work. Not at all. In fact, the first man frowns, grunts something to his mates, leans forward and grabs Marieke's wrists. With one jerk he has her standing on her feet. Marieke gasps, "Hey!" and tries to pull her wrists free to no avail. Where is the guy from the restaurant when you need him?

Chapter 3

The large man spins her around before Marieke has a chance to do anything, something. His tanned hands grip her just above her wrists, pushing them together. She tries to elbow him, but it's like banging her elbow into solid rock, and she pulls a face. The large guy doesn't even seem to notice. She tries stamping on his foot but he simply moves his and blocks her legs. Marieke wracks her brains, thinking back to the few 'self-defence for women' classes she had in secondary school. Poke into someone's eyes. Out. Stomp on their foot. Tried that, didn't work. Scream for help. She takes a deep breath, hears the big guy chuckle, then he simply moves her arm across her stomach, and all the air whooshes out of her lungs. That didn't work either.

Marieke can feel her breath coming faster and faster. Panic is now definitely settling in with a view to stay. She desperately tries to take deeper, calmer breaths. The guy smells of outdoor, sweat and hard work. She tries to wriggle, go down, turn... anything to get free, but nothing helps. Her wrists are pushed together, and one of the other men ties them together with a thin leather strap. Marieke can feel the tears burning, and one slips out, however hard she tries to stay cool and angry, rather than look like a crying, desperate woman. The guys aren't rough or harsh, just calm and firm, but Marieke can feel the first few sobs starting. Her glasses are getting wet. The first guy tries to take them off but changes his mind when he sees her panic. He simply runs his fingers over the rim, and Marieke snaps, "Never seen glasses before or something?" He lowers his eyebrows at her, and she glares back, her mind trying to think of a list of unpleasant things she could do to him. The list isn't very long. He steps back a little, and Marieke looks round, frantically. This is not a joke, and their stag party has taken an unexpected turn. For a second she realises that, unlike any other stag party group, this one doesn't seem to smell like a pub on a late Saturday night.

Her thoughts and feelings are all over the place and Marieke tries to struggle as much as she can when the large guy, who she now calls Eric (good old Viking name) pulls her along towards the rest of the group. The guy that tied her up appears with her large handbag, says something to 'Eric' who slows down, allowing the guy to hang her handbag round her neck. The men pull her hands through and adjust the bag, his fingers stroking down her arm making her shudder. "Thank you," she says, as sarcastically as possible, "how very kind and thoughtful of you." They look at her and shrug. Her struggling doesn't seem to make any difference whatsoever as 'Eric' propels her towards the other guys as if she was running along with him, rather than ruining her boots by trying to dig into the carpet with every step. Marieke looks round for the restaurant man, what was his name? "Ramon?" She calls out, hoping that the fake Vikings will think she is with somebody as well. The big guy 'Eric' spins her round, produces a dirty rag, and waves it at her, saying something at the same time. She doesn't need any translator to know what he means. Marieke swallows, hesitating between nodding demurely or pulling her most defiant face, ending up with a weird mixture of the two.

When they join the main group, Eric says something, and they all start. One of the men looks at Marieke and says something. She has no idea what he said, but his nasty smirk and the way he looks at her makes her shudder. Some of the others laugh as well, but 'Eric' grips her arm just that tiny bit harder and says something in a very definite tone of voice, and the laughter stops. The nasty guy, she calls him Leer from the way he looked at her, looks sulky as if he was told off. Marieke is pushed along the corridor towards the stairs. She looks at the ladies' and wonders if she should say she needs the bathroom, but 'Eric' simply pushes her a bit harder, as if he can guess her idea before she even made it into a proper plan. Soon they reach the staircase, and Marieke, who isn't keen on stairs at the best of times realises how hard it is to get down them with your hands tied. A few times she almost loses her balance, and Eric shakes her and says something.

She glares at him, "You have no idea how hard it is to get down these with my hands tied up. How about you try it yourself," and she would probably have gone on for a while longer, but seeing his face harden, as well as his grip on her arm, she decides the point has been sufficiently made. Her hope lies in the car-deck attendants or other drivers. Surely if they are going to push her into one of their cars, there will still be attendants on deck, as they wouldn't leave as long as some drivers haven't returned to their vehicle, would they? And there is her red Panda as well, surely they would check it all out? The car deck brings a new shock for Marieke. It is totally deserted. The huge doors at the front are wide open, indicating that all the other cars have left the ferry. Marieke looks round for her car, but there is no sign of it. Of course, it might be on the other side of the partition, she has no idea which side she was parked. The group walks towards the open doors, clearly exulted, and Marieke is forced to walk faster as well.

They step outside the ferry, and Marieke gasps, "No! What? How on earth…" Her voice trails off, and she stops, ignoring the quick shake Eric gives her, unaware that he is moving her along again, with Marieke staggering and tripping over her own feet. They have walked onto sand, like a beach, with huge cliff walls ahead of them, the water a dark blue, almost black. The sky is still dark, and the cliffs even darker. No sign of white cliffs, so it's not Dover that they got to. Marieke tries to follow the dark cliffs, but they seem to go on for ever. When she looks back across the water she can see cliffs there as well. It's a narrow gorge, perhaps a river. Did they just hijack a ferry? The air is cold, and she shivers, though not just because of the cold. Before she can stop it, her throat has made a whimpering sound, and 'Eric' turns her round. His hard eyes stare at her for a second, then he lets go of her arm and starts tugging at her coat. His fingers touch her zip, and he frowns. His hands go still for a second, then, with a shrug, he simply pulls the coat tighter around her, adjusts her bag strap to keep it tight, then grabs her arm again.

'Eric' calls out something, and a few of the guys walk towards the dark shapes that Marieke is sure are trees. After a while, they return with armfuls of branches and twigs. They pile up the twigs, and one of the guys kneels in the sand and starts doing something to the pile. Marieke is more and more aware of how cold, tired, annoyed and even bored she is when suddenly a flame appears in the bunch of twigs. The guys say something and some laugh, then they all move closer to the fire. So they were cold too, Marieke thinks, feeling vindictive. Serves them right. But where are we? This is most definitely not Dunkirk, and nowhere near Dunkirk do they have cliffs this high, not along any of the French rivers in Flanders. The air is thin, having a slight frosty feel to it, and she is sure that she can see whiteness on the top, like snow. She hesitates, then turns to 'Eric' and says, "Where are we? Where did you guys take me?" He looks at her, frowns, and shrugs his shoulders. She tries again in Dutch, and even in her best school German, but he simply shrugs again and looks away, calling out something to one of the men.

The man nods, and puts an old fashioned type horn to his mouth, and blows three times, making Marieke's ears ring. She covers one ear with her bound hands, the other one she digs into her shoulder. Eric laughs at her, then says something to the men, pushes her closer to the fire, and suddenly knocks against her legs, making her fall onto the sand. Marieke hits her knee, and cries out, more angry than sore. If she thought he would feel guilty, she realises that she has thought wrong. He doesn't even look at her. For a moment she wonders if she should make her point, then changes her mind. Mainly because Leer is sitting not too far away from her, and she doesn't want to attract his attention.

Chapter 4

Marieke sits down, her knees pulled up close to stay warm. Within seconds she realises the soft beach sand isn't that soft after all and rubs her knee subconsciously. She looks at 'Eric' without turning her head and finds him looking at her. Great. The other men have pulled the loose cloak type garments they are wearing tighter around them. Most of them have their eyes shut and seem to be nodding off. Is this her chance? Her heart beats faster as she tries to move half an inch away from Eric, further back from the fire, slightly further away from him. She keeps her eyes fixed on the bouncing flames, half mesmerized by them.

By the time Marieke manages to shuffle an inch away, she feels Eric's hard hand on her elbow. He leans in a tiny bit and growls, "Nei," then sits back as if nothing has happened. Marieke feels her face heating up, her eyes burning with tears. It seemed such a good idea! For a few seconds, she wonders if she should pretend not to know what 'nei' means, but it sounds like her cousins from Dordt saying 'no' in Dutch and she's not a good liar. She sighs, then lowers her head, pretending to doze off like the others, for Leer has stirred, and he is looking directly at her. His eyes are narrowed, no expression on his face, and for a moment she hopes he is still asleep. The way he suddenly licks his lips makes her shudder. Before Marieke knows it she has carefully shuffled the one inch gain back towards Eric. Somehow she feels safer with him, however grumpy he might seem.

She sighs quietly, finally allowing the tears to come. She really is stuck, with a bunch of Vikings, goodness knows where. She lowers herself as much as possible into her coat, trying to stay quiet. The last thing she wants is more attention from any of these guys. Marieke squeezes her eyes shut, and thinks that now is the time to pray. What should she pray? For Dunkirk to suddenly appear? For the ferry attendants to turn up? For these guys to walk away? The situation is bizarre and only the tight straps around her wrists tell her she is wide awake. She uses the tips of her fingers to wipe away her tears, and dry her glasses. She glances back at the ferry, like a link between normality and nightmare. Marieke is too tired to figure it out; she doesn't even know where to start praying. One thing is sure, she isn't planning on falling asleep. The rest on the ferry has done her good, and the orange and yellow wrestling flames soon dry the tears on her face and the front of her coat.

Slowly the dawn creeps upon them, turning the dark outlines into woods and rocks. Marieke glances round, trying to not draw attention to herself, looking for clues as to where she is. The landscape is wild and impressive, and she would have thoroughly enjoyed it if this was a holiday. The circumstances spoil the scenery though, and soon a sound is added to the view that destroys any peaceful, relaxing feelings she might have had. Horses. Marieke soon spots dozens of horses trotting down a rudimentary road from the forest, that leads steeply down towards them at the beach. There are a few men with the horses, but most are rider-less, all saddled and ready for use. She guesses their use, her heart racing ahead of the rhythm of the horses' hooves. Before Marieke can name the terror each hoofbeat brings her, she feels 'Eric's' hand on her elbow, effortlessly pulling her to her feet. She hardly notices, her eyes drawn to the moving horses coming towards them.

Marieke tries to swallow, licking her dry lips, her lungs doing their best to fill themselves with some fresh morning air, but nothing seems to function. 'Eric' gives her arm a little impatient jerk, but she doesn't even notice. Suddenly he swings her round, breaking her wide-eyed stare at the animals, temporarily pausing the spell as well. He glares at her, then narrows his eyes, his mouth relaxing a little. Marieke manages a big gulp of air, not caring in the slightest that the corners of 'Eric's' mouth have gone down. All she can think about is the horses. Their sound comes nearer, not just their pounding hooves, but the blowing snorts, and she can imagine spraying flecks of foam. She shudders and opens her mouth to protest. But 'Eric' has swung her back round again, ignoring her desperate gasp as she realises how close the horses are. He propels her towards the nearest one, a dark brown horse, huge in Marieke's estimation.

She digs her heels in as much as possible, but it makes no difference. Soon the horse's flanks tower over her, 'Eric's hand on the rope, the other one still on her elbow. "No," she gasps, fighting for all she is worth this time. Blind with fear somehow her kicks miss him completely, the horse swinging its huge head, the dreaded foam landing on her boot. It's a small fleck, but still, Marieke can feel hysterics coming in faster than the tide in Scheveningen. "No, I'm not getting on that, I'm not ever... " She stops, as she finds herself on the horse. 'Eric' has swung himself up, and with a quick flick of his arm, has landed her in front of him. Her scream comes out as a half shriek as she gasps for breath. Marieke's whole body is shaking uncontrollably as she dimly realises that thrashing about on top of a horse is probably not wise. 'Eric' puts a finger on her throat, suddenly blocking all air out completely.

"Nei," he growls in her ear, not loud, not angry, just clear. Then he lets go, and Marieke swallows and coughs, feeling lightheaded with fear. She tries to look at him, she has to look at him for she has to somehow make clear that she can't go on a horse, won't go on a horse. He has to understand. Her eyes struggle to focus on his face, and she ends up shaking her head endlessly, stammering 'Nei' in the best Viking accent possible. 'Eric' looks back at her, lowering his eyelids slightly, then shuffles back a little and pulls her tighter towards him. His rough hands grab hers and push them around a big knob at the front of the saddle. All she can do is cling on. She doesn't dare to kick or fight; he'll simply strangle her again. Her white knuckles clench around the saddle knob, splattered by her tears.

Then the horse starts to move, and Marieke gives a half sob, half shriek. She has to get off. Anything is better than this. She'll have to drop down, now, before 'Eric' realises she has gone limp and starts to slide down the horse. He manages to grab her at the last moment, pulling her back in front of him. Marieke shakes her head at him, trying to say her one Viking word again, but the darkness starts flooding in from the sides. The world moves in circles, faster than the horse. She draws in air, but nothing can stop the overwhelming darkness, and the last thing she sees is the shocked, grey eyes of 'Eric' looking at her.

Chapter 5

Marieke's eyes blink wildly and finally open, then snap shut. This can't be true, it has to be a bad dream, and maybe if she tries again she will find herself back in normality. When she opens her eyes for the second time, nothing has changed. She is still on the back of a moving horse, held by an outdoorsy smelling Viking. 'Eric' pulls her up a little higher, half turning her away from the horse's head. It feels like they're flying and Marieke simply closes her eyes and sobs.

One cannot cry forever though, and Marieke eventually stops crying ad concentrates on controlling the queasiness that rises with every bounce and jolt. She knows if she looks at the bushes and tall pine tress whizzing past she will feel seasick. Rider sick. Whichever, she will be sick. So she closes her eyes and breathes slowly and deeply. For a moment she feels that maybe being sick all over 'Eric' will serve him right, but somehow she knows it won't help in the long run. Every now and again she squints through her eyelashes. Still trees and a rough road, still going uphill at a constant speed.

Finally, the horses slow down a little, and Marieke can sense they are on a steeper climb. It feels precarious, and she clamps her lips together to stop herself from squealing or crying. Tears slip down again. She doesn't care where the Vikings are going anymore, as long as it's somewhere off this horse. She wipes her face on her shoulder, rather tempted to do it on his rough shirt. 'Eric' nudges her and she looks up at him through wet glasses. She attempts an angry, defiant glare, which he ignores as he nods up ahead. She follows his look and spots a large grey stone castle rising from the forest. The forest seems dark, menacing and the castle grim.

Part of her is relieved that the horse ride might end soon. She bites her lip though, for her confusion is becoming overwhelming. The horses and castle are over the top for a stag do that has gotten out of hand. So where is this, and what is going on? Will the castle be a hotel? Or just the end, and they'll explain it was all for laughs, and take her back? Deep down, she senses this is no setup or party. It feels like a terrible joke. Her head aches, her eyes are sore and her back and bottom hurt and feel bruised.

All too soon the castle looms up huge and forbidding, and Marieke wonders if she should have another go at sliding off the horse before they get to the castle. As her whole body is shaking and she has no idea where they are, she realises it isn't an option. The horses' hooves make a dreadful racket crossing the wooden drawbridge, and then they arrive in a large courtyard. Marieke tries to take in the sights and noises through her stained glasses; the imposing entranceway, hard-faced watchmen glancing up to see them arrive. The horse stops, and 'Eric' slides off, dragging her down with him as a groom takes the reigns. She gasps and tries to cry out, but his hand round her throat, and an angry, "Hysj" stops her. He grabs her around her waist, pinning her arms to her side, and carries her very quickly to a corner of the courtyard. It's dark, but as they get closer Marieke spots a large stone staircase. He almost seems to run up the steps to enter a dark corridor lit by a smoky torch, the loud men's noises fading away.

At the end of the long, chilly corridor is a sturdy looking wooden door. 'Eric' raps on the door, then opens it. Once through, he puts Marieke down, holding on to her elbow, and pulls her along with him, slower now. It looks like an apartment hall, with various doors leading off to the sides. Again 'Eric' knocks on a door, opens it, and pushes her through. She enters a good-sized living room, with a fire burning in a large fireplace. Several women are seated around the fire, and Marieke shivers. A man steps forward, and Marieke notices his limp and sulky face, but he bows his head respectfully to 'Eric' and says something that seems a greeting, his eyes gleaming as he looks Marieke up and down. Eric says quite a lot in return, nodding towards Marieke now and then. The man frowns, looking even sulkier, his eyes dark. Marieke has a feeling he has just been told to look after her, and he's not happy with the job. Well, she's not happy either. Especially not as he looks her over again, more obvious this time, and says something to 'Eric', and the two men laugh.

Some of the women have joined her sulky minder, and when 'Eric' says something to them they nod and smile. The women aren't tall but elegant, their long hair tied up over their heads with ribbons matching their fine long dresses. Marieke can feel her face glowing as eyes stare at her. Then 'Eric' swings her around, and undoes the straps around her wrist. Marieke rubs her wrists, where red and white criss-cross lines stand up in a careless relief pattern. She glares at him, but that doesn't seem to get through. Marieke scans the room, looking for other ways out. The sulky man edges a little closer to her, and Marieke gives a tiny shudder. It's the way he looks at her, licking his lips, and she tries to put as much anger in her eyes as she can.

'Eric' says something to him and he shrugs, but he moves back, making Marieke breathe easier. So 'Eric' has a lot to say in this place as well. A dark-haired women returns from a side door, and nods to a blond-haired woman. The blond one takes Marieke's arm, not harshly, just round her elbow, like you would with a friend. Marieke hesitates. The woman smiles a little, sympathy glowing in her eyes. The darker one that came through the door joins on Marieke's other side, accidentally nudging the sulky man out of the way. His sulk deepens, and Marieke suddenly feels more inclined to go with these two. She follows them through the door, briefly noticing the beautiful carvings in the dark wood.

Chapter 6

The two women bring Marieke into some kind of bathroom. There is a large wooden bowl on a table, with a folded cloth next to it. A smaller cloth is hanging on the rim of the bowl, and a block of some kind is next to the large cloth. The blond woman guides her to the bowl, points at the various articles, and her one free hand moves as fast as her words. Marieke is sure that the smaller cloth is a facecloth, and the block is soap. When the woman flaps her hand towards a beautiful horn comb, Marieke nods, keeping her face neutral. A comb? For her hair? Her frizzy hair? The blond woman then giggles, obviously coming to the same conclusion, as her finger tips touch Marieke's hair. Marieke hates strangers touching her hair. But this woman is so clearly intrigued and seems so sweet, she lets her. She holds her own almost platinum blond, straight braid next to Marieke's hair, and laughs again.

The dark-haired woman says something, and the blond one drops her braid, blushing a little. Soon, however, she finds another novelty, Marieke's glasses. Gingerly touching the rim with her finger tips, she looks so curious that Marieke rolls her eyes, and takes her glasses off, wiping them very quickly on her coat lining, ashamed of the salty splatters. She holds them towards the woman's face, who peers through them, and gives a shrill gasp. The dark-haired woman forgets herself and comes forward too. Marieke doesn't let go of her glasses, not that she doesn't trust the women. The problem is, she won't be able to see her glasses without them on. Having to feel around for them, hoping to see their hands clearly enough, should they hold out the glasses towards her, would be too embarrassing. She puts her glasses back on and smiles at the women. They look at her as if she's some magician. Both smile at her and Marieke smiles back with some difficulty. Why is she even nice to them? They're the enemy, aren't they? They are helping to keep her here. Granted, they couldn't do much else with 'Eric' around, but on the other hand, none of the women seemed to have objected to 'Eric' delivering her as a captive.

Marieke takes a deep breath and carries on looking around, having already noticed that there is only one door. The toilet is set in the wall and looks very rudimentary, but at least they have one, Marieke thinks. Then the women leave, after giving her one more encouraging smile. The solid door shuts, and suddenly Marieke's legs start to shake, and she lowers herself on the wooden toilet plank, unable to stand any longer. Feeling safer in this room, she takes her glasses off again and cries. When she runs out of tears she wipes her face dry, then walks to the washbowl. She hesitates over the soap. It's ultra-natural of course, but still, will it dry out her skin? In the end, she decides to use a little. The smell is not unpleasant, and it does make her skin feel clean. The water isn't freezing cold as she expected, but a lovely warm temperature. After a good wash, Marieke feels a lot better.

She uses her fingers to tidy up her hair, peering into her tiny mirror. In the depths of her handbag, she finds some lipstick. It's one of those freebies, in a colour which Marieke calls '1950's pink'. She can't remember ever wearing it, as she doesn't normally wear makeup. She always forgets that she has lipstick on, then licks her lips and is reminded in a rather nasty way. This time she feels the bright pink might give her that tiny bit extra confidence.

Done. Should she leave this room, and join the others? She doesn't particularly want to. She hesitates, wandering round the rather small room. Is there really no way out? There is only the tiniest window slit, it hardly lets her hand through, let alone anything else. When she gets close to the door she spots the large old fashioned looking key in the door. In a sudden impulse, she pulls the key out and stuffs it deep down in her handbag. After all, it might come in handy. She tries to look out of the tiny slit window, but the angle is all wrong so Marieke can't see anything, apart from the rather grey sky. She tries to pray, but her thoughts are such a jumble, she doesn't even know where to start or what to say, beyond: "Please let me out of here, Lord!"

There is a knock on the door, which opens a little. The blond lady pops her head through the crack, smiling at Marieke. Marieke smiles back at her, after all, it's not her fault that she is brought here by 'Eric', and maybe she can persuade the women to help her get away. She follows the woman back to the room with the fire. She points to a table with a plate at the other end of the room. When she sits down on the elaborately carved chair, she almost thinks it's naan bread on the plate, then realises it's more like pitta bread. The woman points and nods then joins the other women around the fire. The sulky man is not in the room, and 'Eric' has gone as well. Marieke nibbles the bread, definitely not naan, and coarser than pitta, but not unpleasant. She tries some cheese, rather hard and salty, and takes a tiny sip of the drink. Ugh, lager! Not very strong, but it tastes like mouldy bread, and what the Dutch call a 'brown cafe'. She shudders, wishing she had left her water bottle in her bag. Her water bottle however is in the car, as she doesn't like carrying it in her handbag in case it spills.

The darker haired woman comes to see if she is alright, and Marieke decides to ask for water. She smiles at the woman, and says, "Can I have water?" She makes a drinking sign, then says the word water in every possible dialect. The woman looks blank, her eyes intense, as she is trying to understand. In the end, she nods, leaves the room, and soon returns with another crude glass mug, this one filled with water. Marieke is relieved, smiles at her and says, "Thank you," and fishes her painkillers from her bag. She needs to get on top of this headache before it gets worse. After eating her fill she leans back in the wooden chair, and studies the room. Thick curtains line the small windows. The windows have some translucent material, but Marieke can't tell whether it's glass or not. There is a lot of wood around the room, mostly beautifully carved, like the furniture. Marieke likes the chair she sits on. It looks like a proper Viking chair, she decides, running her fingertip around the carved out dragons on the arms.

The blond woman comes over to where Marieke sits, just as the sulky man enters the room. He says something to the blond woman, who turns round and answers him. He scowls, and the woman turns back to Marieke, but Marieke just catches the woman rolling her eyes to herself. So the sulky man isn't popular, or did he say something wrong? He comes closer and speaks to Marieke, but she has no idea what he wants from her. She shrugs and makes a sleeping hand sign, resting her face on her put together hands. The blond woman smiles and nods. The man looks out of the window and says something, his lips curled in a snarl. Marieke is the one that rolls her eyes this time. "I know it's daytime, but I have been up most of the night, you know," sounding waspish, knowing the guy won't understand her words. He clearly understands her attitude though and narrows his eyes at her as he steps closer in a menacing gesture. Marieke is frozen like a deer in the headlights, but the blond woman quickly steps between them, saying something in a soothing voice as she pulls Marieke by her elbow again. Marieke grabs her handbag and follows the blond woman, careful not to look at him. She is suddenly frightened, shocked by his reaction to her words. Maybe she was pushing her luck talking to him like that and openly rolling her eyes at him. What if he comes to get revenge; teach her a lesson?

Chapter 7

Marieke follows the blond woman along the main corridor again, trying to count doors, and soon they stop outside another wooden door. The woman opens it, and Marieke suddenly finds herself overcome with curiosity. Did Vikings have four-poster beds? Turns out they didn't, at least this room doesn't. The bed is small and the room is simple, with another small window and the same dark curtains. The blond woman motions towards the bed, points out another bowl and pitcher, smiles, and leaves the room, the latch dropping in place. Marieke hesitates a moment, holding on to her handbag, eyeing up the room. Remembering her minder's vicious look, she digs in her handbag to retrieve the large key. Softly she walks to the door. Yes, there is a keyhole, but no key. She pokes the key from her handbag in the slot and turns the lock. It works! The lock grinds into place.

She leaves the key in the door and lowers herself on the bed. The next dilemma is her glasses. Does she sleep with them on, as she did on the boat, or should she take them off? Sleeping with her glasses on is very uncomfortable, but they're worth a fortune, so she can't lose them. Taking them off means she is hardly able to see a thing. She will have to feel for them, and if she is woken up in a hurry that could be a problem. Also, what if somebody manages to get in whilst she is asleep, and take her glasses…she'd be sunk! She needs to rest, then make a plan to get out of here, where ever 'here' is.

Marieke lies down on the rough sheets and woollen blanket, not bothering to get into bed properly. She is tired but wide awake, and she knows if she sleeps too well, there'll be trouble tonight. Plus, she will wake up groggy. Her thoughts are spinning in several directions at once, making her feel queasy with the stress of it all. What has happened? Obviously, it's not a deranged Stag do, but what then? Are they some weird hippy group? Her headache hasn't improved from the tablets she took earlier, and Marieke closes her eyes, feeling panic creeping up on her. A soft noise makes her eyes fly open, and she looks around to see what it is. Her look falls on the door handle, a large metal ring. It is turning ever so slowly, making a very soft grinding noise. Marieke holds her breath, smirking at the same time. Will the lock hold?

The handle stops moving, and Marieke is sure that the door is being pushed. Nothing happens, the lock holds and after a while, the handle turns back carefully. Marieke listens as intently as possible, her smirk much bigger now, wondering if she should slip off the bed to listen at the door. She is pretty sure she can hear soft footsteps disappearing down the corridor, so she stays where she is. Who was it? Suddenly she changes her mind, jumps off the bed and tiptoes to the door. She turns the key as noiselessly as possible, cringing at the creaking metal. Then she turns the handle, pulls the door open, and peeps through a crack. She is just in time to see her sulky minder disappear into a door at the far end of the corridor, presumably the living room. Should she try to escape now, knowing he is in that room? She remembers the larger, carved door right at the end of the corridor leads to the outer courtyard. Suddenly her escape plan falls as she realises there will still be many people in the courtyard.

Marieke shuts the door, locks it carefully, and returns to the bed. Did he just want to check she was alright? But why the sneakiness? Surely if he simply came to see if she needed anything else, he would have knocked, and opened the door in a normal way? She stares at the white washed ceiling with its dark wooden beams. A thought enters her head and she gets quickly off the bed, unlocks the door, and puts the key into her handbag. If they know she has locked it, they will take away the key and Marieke is keen to hang onto her key. Who knows how useful it might be? Soon sleep overtakes her. This time she doesn't hear the door handle being turned and fails to notice the dark-haired woman gaze at her through the door. The door closes again, but Marieke sleeps on.

When Marieke wakes up, the room is more shadowy than before. She groans, feeling as groggy as she knew she would. Her head throbs and her mouth is dry. She walks to the wooden basin and pours herself a glass of water from the large pitcher. Her legs are wobbly, and she is glad to sit on the edge of her bed. After some water and recovery time, she feels better. Not great, but alright. She washes her face, and just as she is drying her hands, wondering what her next move should be, there is a knock on the door, and the kind, blond woman puts her head round the door. She smiles at Marieke and beckons her to follow her. Marieke hopes there will be food, as she is hungry.

There is food, Marieke sees to her relief when the blond woman leads her to another room (How is she going to find her way around all these identical looking doors?). There is a large dining table, and she sees the dark-haired woman, 'Eric', her sulky minder and a few others that she recognises from this morning. She glares at them all, but they don't pay her much attention. The table is covered in a linen cloth with embroidery, earthenware plates, glasses in different colours and knives. Marieke is shown a seat, and her fingers automatically touch the knife. When she looks up she finds 'Eric' looking at her, a slightly sarcastic smile on his face. She blushes. Did he think she was going to attack them all with this knife? Although, if she could smuggle the knife out after the meal, who knows how it might come in handy. She deliberately keeps her hand well away from the knife, in case she has a chance to take it later. The more Marieke thinks about it, the more she likes the idea of having some kind of weapon. Just in case. Then she smiles wryly to herself as she realises she has neither the skill nor the inclination to use it.

As Marieke looks around the table, she finds the woman next to 'Eric' glaring at her. Her yellow blonde hair lies in flat plaits and the corners of her large mouth are turned down. Marieke can see from the lines around the woman's mouth that this is its natural position. The woman's plain dress is brightened up with several strings of bright coloured glass beads and two gold brooches, one just under each shoulder. Marieke can feel her stomach tightening, the warmth in her face growing, and she forces herself to remember that this is not the first time somebody has glared at her. The woman is probably hungry. 'Eric' sees what she is looking at, and leans over to the woman, and as he says something, her eyes do not leave Marieke's face. The woman instantly cheers up, and smiles, albeit unpleasantly. The sulky man must have overheard, for he makes a surprisingly similar smile. Marieke shivers, with a nasty sense of foreboding, a tiny voice whispering in her head wondering why 'Eric' has brought her here.

The meal is surprisingly good. The vegetables are the conserved type, rather than fresh, but this doesn't detract from their flavour. The meat tastes like chicken, but Marieke doesn't want to ask, in case it isn't. She glances around the table, hoping to see at least some salt, but no, nothing. Not having a fork is awkward, and she doesn't want to use her fingers like some of the others. Eating with just a knife is like eating in a Chinese restaurant with only one chopstick, but she manages. The drink seems to be lager again, and Marieke wonders what to do. She can't see herself drinking a whole glass of lager, but how does she ask for water? In the end, she has just a few sips, hoping to get more water when she's back in her room.

When the meal is over, the dark-haired woman walks up to her and smiles. She points at herself, and says, "Erika", her voice calm and soothing somehow. Marieke smiles back and says her own name. Erika nods and repeats her name. She takes Marieke by her elbow, and guides her to the blond woman, points at her and says, "Gunilla". Marieke smiles at her, and nods. Gunilla repeats Marieke's name, and the three of them leave the dining room. Does this mean she is friends with them? Would they help her to leave the castle, she wonders, following her friends down the corridor and through another door, feeling like Alice in Wonderland with all the doors around her.

Chapter 8

This door leads to the sitting room she was in before, and Marieke pulls a face at herself that she hadn't even recognised it. She watches Gunilla get a cloak-like shawl, and then the three leave the room and go out of the door at the end of the corridor. Marieke follows down the stone corridor in the dim evening light, the smoking torches casting flickering shadows on the walls. Down the stone steps, but staying close to the wall the two Viking women lead her through another plain door.

The room they enter is cold but airy. Several barred windows are letting in plenty of cold air, as well as light. Large wooden tubs take up a lot of floor space with plain wooden tables underneath the windows, and Marieke can tell it must be the laundry room. Erika calls over a young girl with a plain face, her dark blond hair in a simple plait. She looks at them and Erika explains something to her. The girl looks Marieke up and down, nods at Erika then looks back at Marieke. Marieke doesn't even bother with a fake smile, feeling annoyance growing at a very rapid pace. Why did Gunilla and Erika bring her here to be gawked at by another girl? The girl answers Erika, nods and finally Erika smiles at Marieke, points to the girl and says, "Ingeborg", her voice making it clear that Ingeborg is not a friend, but a nice person nonetheless. Marieke nods at Ingeborg, and determined to show that to her all people are equal and that she treats servants like normal human beings, she smiles at Ingeborg. After all, it's not Ingeborg's fault that Gunilla and Erika have dragged her here. Erika's face has gone a little tighter, she notices, and Ingeborg looks uncomfortable. Well, she'll show people how things are done in the 21st century.

"Nice to meet you," she says to the girl, trying to smile rather than look smug, and to her shock, Ingeborg dips down into a curtsy and says, "Tank ee." Both Erika and Gunilla gasp a little, and Marieke feels excited, her head spinning with the implications, her eyes wide. Ingeborg understands her? Well, can she explain the misunderstandings and get her back to her car? Could this mean all troubles can be cleared up? Will Ingeborg speak to 'Eric' and say… Erika's voice is rather sharp as she questions Ingeborg. She looks satisfied once the girl speaks to her, and Ingeborg turns to Marieke, her light blue eyes searching her brain it seems. "I help. Ee ask, I help. I tell, ee do."

Marieke nods, then hesitates; does the girl mean she has to take her orders from her? Do they really think she will work as a slave girl, just like that? Her heart beats faster, and she makes herself as tall as possible, ready to put things straight. This one will have to be cleared up at once, without making matters worse. Was that why 'Eric' was smirking at the table with that woman? He simply brought her here as a slave? Ingeborg however has turned back to the others, saying something that sounds like "traelinna", and they nod. Ingeborg frowns. "I do what exactly?" Marieke asks, but before Ingeborg can answer, Gunilla takes Marieke by her elbow again, and Ingeborg walks away. She suddenly turns around again, and says, "Bee!" Marieke smiles back with difficulty, her mouth struggling to keep up with the suddenness of it all, and says, "Yes, bye. Oh, and thank you!" Is she not going to work with the girl after all?

The three young women go back up the stairs, Marieke having a very quick look around the courtyard. It's shadowy in some places already, and she notices Erika looking round too, her shoulders rigid. She can hear loud metallic banging from one corner, and just across from the stairs must be the stables. A horse snorts loudly, and Marieke walks upstairs a little faster. Back in the sitting room, the girls show her to one of the beautifully carved chairs in front of the fire, and Marieke rubs her hands together, stretching them towards the hearth. She plays with a loose strand of her hair, worried about tomorrow morning. How is she going to wash her hair without her special shampoo? Would 'Eric' go to her car on the ferry to retrieve her suitcase? Could she ask Ingeborg to translate for her? It was all too ridiculous for words.

The door opens, and the grumpy woman walks in with 'Eric' and the minder. Two other women follow, girls really, who hardly look at Marieke. Their dresses are almost as plain as the grumpy woman's, and their hair is the same kind of yellow. The girls go to the table near the window and set up what looks like a board game. For one absurd moment, Marieke feels relieved that they won't have Monopoly, so no endless hours on one game needed. As if it's anything to do with her. Not that she wants to play a board game with these people, for every time she looks at them smiling at her, she wonders how they can be pretending to be friendly whilst keeping her a prisoner at the same time. By not speaking up on her behalf, they have become part of the problem. Isn't that always how people end up oppressed? It's the majority of people not speaking up. She looks away from the girls, her eyes stinging with tears at the injustice of it all.

The grumpy woman says something to 'Eric' who holds her hand, clearly saying goodbye. Her voice is a bit coarse and whiny, and when 'Eric' is gone she turns to Marieke and the other two. Again the whiny voice, and this time she glares openly at Marieke, who glares back. She might have only seen the woman once, but already Marieke has decided she can't stand her. A tiny sliver of guilt digs into her conscience, but Marieke defends herself by arguing that the woman has been against her ever since they saw each other. She had looked at her then in a nasty way and only cheered up when 'Eric' had said something unkind, of that she is sure.

The minder chuckles, which doesn't do much to cheer her up. The woman snaps something at him and his mouth turns down. His limp seems more obvious as he walks over to the girls at the window. Gunilla and Erika look uncomfortable, and Gunilla has her hands gripping her pretty dress. She looks like she is going to say something, but Erika nudges her with her knee. She says something to the grumpy woman in her calm voice, a bit slower than usual, Marieke thinks, wondering what the Viking word for 'patronising' is.

Erika smiles at Marieke, her eyes looking a little worried, then gestures to the yellow-haired woman and says, "Hillevi", then links her fingers together, points to the door and says, "Harald". Does she mean Hillevi is married to Harald? Marieke feels sheer annoyance that her 'Eric' is called Harald. How disappointing! And Hillevi! How appropriate, she almost

35

chuckles to herself, thinking of the Dutch slang word for a scolding woman, 'Helleveeg', literally a Hell sweep. Instead, she inclines her head to the woman, giving a rather demure smile, guessing that a happy one won't go down well. The woman rolls her eyes at her, looking her up and down, and even tuts when seeing the little bit of leg between Marieke's dress and her leather boots. Marieke feels her face glowing again, the roots of her hair itching, not in the least inclined to smile anymore. She shifts a little in her chair, deliberately looking away from Hillevi, after giving her a last contemptuous glance. After all, two can play that game. Her cheeks burn even more, with shame this time as she realises she's in the wrong. Why should she return Hillevi's nastiness with the same, knowing that two wrongs don't make a right? She thinks of her Christian heroes over the centuries who have returned bad with good. Even if the people aren't real? Aren't they real though? Marieke shuffles uncomfortably in her chair, avoiding Hillevi. Hillevi sits down at a rather small but ornate loom, half-turned away from the three around the fire, and Marieke feels relieved. When she starts weaving, Gunilla smiles brightly at Marieke, rolls her eyes, and shrugs. Marieke grins back, still way too amused over the unfortunate name to stay cross with Hillevi, and glad she isn't the only one who seems to dislike her. She ought to know better though, the tiny sliver in her conscience brightening with each colourful spark in the fireplace.

Chapter 9

Erika and Gunilla chat quietly, Hillevi works on the loom, the young girls play their game, and Marieke simply stares at the flames, tired from it all, anger making her heart beat faster. Having met Ingeborg gives her a little hope, but the whole situation is mad. The room becomes darker, and a man comes in quietly to light a few candles around the room. The others don't even look at him, but Marieke smiles at him to show her thanks, as well as set an example. The man glares back, and Erika actually nudges her with her foot! Marieke scowls into the flames and yawns. How long does it take to show people a better way, one without oppression or discrimination?

Just then, Ingeborg comes in with a pile of linen. She simply waits at the door, and the minder comes over. He beckons Marieke, looking more cross than ever. She hesitates for a moment and glances at Erika and Gunilla. They smile and nod at her, so she gets up and follows him out of the door. He takes her and Ingeborg back to her bedroom, then leaves them to it. Ingeborg smiles at her shyly and lays the clothes on her bed one by one. The first is a very simply off-white dress. "Slepping," she says and Marieke nods, yes, it does look like a nightdress. The other dresses are prettier, some with embroidery, some striped. There are two woollen cloaks, and Ingeborg produces two brooches to pin them on with. Marieke smiles at her, and thanks her. "Pleas," says Ingeborg, proud of her ability to communicate.

Marieke hesitates, should she ask Ingeborg to help her to get out? There is a cough at the door, and Ingeborg shrinks down a little. The minder has silently returned and says something to her, making her blush, and after a very quick curtsy, and a "Bee," she leaves the room. Marieke lets go of the breath she didn't know she'd been holding in and feels cheated of her chance to escape. She turns to glare at sulky guy, but he has already left. She stands at the door, drilling her eyes into his retreating back, wishing it was the dinner knife instead, wondering whether to return to the living room or not. Just then she spots Hillevi walking down the corridor, followed again by the two young girls. Seems it's bedtime then. She shrinks back a little, not wanting to be glared at again, and not trusting her own looks to be pleasant either. She closes the door slowly. She decides to lock it again, and just hearing the key grind in the lock makes her feel safer.

Her phone still has a little bit of battery, but still no signal, not even near the window. Marieke had tried in the bathroom this morning and had hoped that it was to do with the walls or position of the bathroom. Not even an emergency contact is at the top. She dials 999, then 112, wondering what number is used by Scandinavian countries, but the phone doesn't help at all. None of the numbers are recognised. Marieke swallows, feeling suddenly very lonely and cut off. Her mum didn't know she was supposed to be coming, so won't be worried; her colleagues think she's having a wonderful holiday, so they won't worry either when she doesn't turn up for work. Anyway, how would they ever find her? She switches her phone off, maybe the battery will last long enough for her to get out of the castle, switch it back on and call for help. Imagining the 999 call makes her grin a little, "Yes officer, I need someone to deal with these Vikings that kidnapped me, and they need to feel the full force of the law!" Maybe she should start a petition to bring back capital punishment.

The grin is replaced by tears, as Marieke sobs, her face buried in one of the woollen cloaks. When she's done she takes her glasses off, mops her face dry with her sleeve, and takes stock. She has a nighty, a few dresses and two cloaks. That will do for now. She wished she could Google natural soap and frizzy hair. Or, how to escape a Viking castle. She folds the dresses up and puts them on a low bench for now. Marieke grabs her handbag and coat, and tiptoes to her door, unlocks it and peeps out. All is quiet.

She steps out into the corridor and hesitates. Should she lock her door, so they won't find out that she has gone? In the end, she decides against it and walks as quietly as possible down the long corridor, which seems to get longer with each furtive step. Her eyes are fixed on the carved door at the end, and although she still has the entire castle to escape from, that door somehow signals the first step to freedom. Just as she turns the ring, holding her breath in case it squeaks, she hears a noise behind her. Before she has a chance to look behind her, rough hands grab her shoulders and spin her round, slamming her back into the door. The door is definitely solid. Marieke gasps, forcing the cry of pain to stay inside. It's her minder who manages to combine sulky and triumphant into one nasty look. He growls at her, obviously pleased with himself, despising her, and Marieke says, "I have no idea what you're saying, I was just going for a walk. I needed some fresh air, as I have been inside most of the day. Now please let me go."

The result is that he slams her back into the door again, not as hard as the first time, but Marieke gasps and glares at him with teary eyes. He glares, opens his mouth to tell her off again, but hearing another door open shrugs, and simply says, "Nei," whilst pushing her past him towards her allocated bedroom. Through blurry eyes Marieke sees Erika standing in the door opening of her room, looking concerned. She says something sharp to him. He answers roughly, stepping closer to Erika. Marieke watches the two, wondering wildly if she should try again, and run past now, but no, that would be utterly pointless. She rubs her back and sees how her sulky minder steps away from Erika as soon as the young woman says something sharp, mentioning Harald. He turns round, sees Marieke staring at them, and advances, his eyes hard and menacing. Marieke decides that sleep might actually be a good thing right now. After a last thankful glance at Erka, she walks down the corridor to her room, glad she didn't lock the door after all.

She shuts the door with a bang, drops her bag, pulls her coat off with wild movements, her hands shaking. Pure anger, she tells herself. She gets into the Viking nightdress, twisting her neck to try and see if her back is bruised. It feels like it. The brute, he could have merely stopped her, there was no need to bash her like that. She bets he enjoyed that little moment of power. She'll remember that, and next time she'll have to use speed as he might not be able to outrun her. She is determined to get away from this place. She brushes her teeth with her finger, hesitates and decides to wash her tights and undies and let them dry overnight. The blanket feels nice and heavy, her pillow soon wet as Marieke cries herself to sleep.

Marieke wakes up and looks at the white ceiling with the dark beams above her head. Her legs feel stiff from sleeping on a short bed. She rubs her face and sighs. She forgot her cream last night. The room is cold, the fire went out at some time in the night. Was she supposed to look after it? She gets up, her back sore and hobbles to the fireplace. When she blows softly on the grey embers, a tiny glow appears. Marieke keeps blowing, adding a very small twig to the red glow. By the time she feels she might begin hyperventilating the twig catches on, and soon the bigger log is burning too. Marieke stays hunched up near the fire, drinking in the warmth as well as the smoke. She rakes her fingers through her hair with difficulty and decides against washing it. It will dry her hair out too much. Feeling cramped from sitting in an awkward position for too long, Marieke decides to get dressed. She puts on one of her new Viking dresses.

The dress is surprisingly soft, the yellow and reds cheerful, and the embroidery along the hem and end of the sleeves pretty. The dress is long but doesn't feel too heavy. The cut isn't particularly fashionable, and totally unsuited for her body shape, but she expects none of her friends will see her today. Marieke can feel her eyes sting, and she walks briskly to her bag to retrieve her small tub of coconut oil. She hesitates. How long will it need to last her? She rubs a tiny amount on her face and an even tinier amount on her hair endings. Rubbing her fingers clean on the palm of her hand she then rubs her hands all over her hair. There. That should do it.

She tries to look out of the window, but the slit is so narrow, she can't make anything out, apart from a grey sky. She leans her forehead against the cold stone, tears blurring the grey even more. "I want to go home, Lord, I just want to get back to normal! I hate these people, and how they make me feel, and although the two women and Ingeborg seem nice, they're still part of the system keeping me here. Nobody is helping me, and I have no one to trust or even talk to. Nobody looks like me, nothing is right, the food is wrong, the drink is gross, even this dress isn't the right shape for me, and…" Yes, she knows she's having a proper pity party, but surely she is entitled to one? Her circumstances are plain awful, and she is totally on her own. It was not a situation she could accept and looking for bright spots, counting her blessings seemed ridiculous. She'd rather count the minutes till she's out of here! Daniel springs to mind, and the sliver of guilt shines brighter. "He wasn't alone though, was he," Marieke hisses out loud, hoping the sliver will be cut back to size.

Chapter 10

arieke's minder bangs on the door, and opens it, looking at her with a smirk. Marieke is glad she hid the key earlier and pushes past him in what she hoped is rude in any culture. He grabs her arm and forces her to walk behind him. Seething she follows him down the corridor to the dining room, back to Hillevi's glaring stare. Harald is there, and he nods, his eyes travelling up and down her dress, but Marieke looks as frosty as she can. Gunilla smiles her bright smile and Erika smiles, patting the chair next to her. Marieke smiles at them, even Hillevi, hoping burning coals are being heaped up on them. Her jaws ache with the effort. Marieke is determined to keep a calm, low profile, as it will make getting out easier.

After breakfast, Erika and Gunilla lead her out of the door quickly, and pull her along to the door leading out of the private apartment area, as Marieke calls it in her mind. Gunilla giggles happily once the door shuts behind them, Erika merely smiles but keeps looking over her shoulder. For a few seconds, Marieke wonders if they're trying to smuggle her out of the castle. Then she realises they're merely giving her a tour of the place, and disappointment makes her eyes mist over. Erika wants to go to the stables first, but Marieke waves her hands in front in what she hopes is a universal sign of No, Not Ever. It works, and although her friends look a little surprised, they give the stables a miss. Erika smiles sympathetically at Marieke, as she is clearly shaken by the thought of having to go close to horses again. At least the horses are still here, so that part was not a dream. Was the ferry a dream? Her little red car? The sharp smell coming from the stable is real enough, and again Marieke decides that this can't be a dream, no matter how much she wishes it was.

Marieke is amazed at how much goes on in a castle. There is coming and going across the drawbridge as well, mainly farmers with carts. Whenever she tries to veer towards the exit, the girls hold her back though. "Nei," says Erika, looking over her shoulder again. "Harald," and she makes a cutting her head off sign with a smile. Marieke nods and smiles back as bright as she possibly can, suppressing the shudder, angry again by their complicity. They go up to the battlements, and Marieke gasps in delight at the incredible view, forgetting her anger for a moment. Forests stretch out as far as she can see, a mix of dark pinewoods, and the green of broadleaf trees in bud. Far in the distance is water; possibly a fjord, blue and mysterious, stretching away into the distance, surrounded by cliffs. It is quiet outside the castle, and the rough grey stones of the battlement are warm under her hands already. She breathes in deeply, the air cold but clean and refreshing. The blue water works like a magnet, her eyes unable to let go, and Marieke feels that if only she could get to the fjord, she'd be free. She screws up her eyes, hoping to spot the ferry beached in the fjord, but there is no sign of it. Her eyes sting, looking at the view, but she makes sure her mouth stays in a bright smile, taking deep, calming breaths, to subdue the little sobs working their way up her throat.

The two women smile at her obvious delight, and after a while they walk on, all the way around the large battlement, passing occasional guards. Marieke notices that there aren't that many guards, and hope bubbles up in her heart. Behind the castle are some open fields with men practising swordplay, and in the distance, Marieke spots more houses with lands. They must be the farms that supply the castle and probably best avoided if she were to escape. They return to the apartments, and the first person they see is Hillevi. Her eyes angrier than ever, her hands tightly clenched, she rattles off a string of harsh-sounding words at Gunilla and Erika, occasionally gesturing towards Marieke. Gunilla frowns and opens her mouth, but Erika is quicker. She holds out a hand in a calming gesture and using a very calm voice, answers Hillevi. The answer takes the heat out of Hillevi's face, but her eyes stay angry. She looks Marieke up and down with a contemptuous expression, but Marieke keeps her face pleasant, even though she feels like saying something equally sharp to the woman. A soft answer does turn away wrath, it appears, as in the end Hillevi shrugs, using that same word 'traelinna' that Ingeborg used, whilst turning away. Erika blows out air, and Gunilla gives a nervous giggle. Erika looks at Marieke, and says, "Harald," with a shrug, rolling her eyes. Marieke bites her lip. Clearly, Harald had not been impressed with her absence? Good, she is not impressed with her presence in this castle, so hopefully, he gets fed up and lets her go. She wonders about the word two women have used now.

Just then her minder comes out of the living room, and the whole conversation is repeated, Marieke realises. Again it is

Erika that answers, whilst Gunilla edges a tiny bit closer to Marieke, and squeezes her hand. Her grey eyes are darker, almost like a stormy sea, and Marieke squeezes her back a little. In the end, her minder returns to the living room, and the two women sigh with relief. They take Marieke along with them to another room. This room is light, with a large fire. There are a few spinning wheels, and Marieke spots a cloth with partial embroidery done. The two young girls she saw last night are sat down already, and they look up. One of them says something with a giggle, and Gunilla answers with a snort. Erika merely rolls her eyes. By the time dinner is served Marieke has learned to spin. Just.

Harald looks marginally more grumpy at dinner time, but Marieke isn't sure if that is because of her castle tour. As she is famished, she doesn't care either. Having only two meals a day is a change to her habits but maybe it will bring a blessing to count, she supposes. She is tired, her back aches, and as they sit in the living room after dinner she stares at the flames, trying to run through Bible verses to comfort herself. Maybe one ought to pray for their enemies, but she can't bring herself to do that. After all, are these people even real? They have no right to keep her here, and who knows for how long. She prays they will let her go soon, and that those that were kind will be blessed, knowing that isn't the right attitude, but she tells herself she can't really pray for them all. Anyway, as they're still in the middle of kidnapping her, she can't very well pray for forgiveness for them, can she? Feeling uncomfortable, she decides that she'd better go to bed before her thoughts make her feel worse.

It turns out Viking life isn't that exciting. At least, not for the women. The men seem to leave the castle regularly, often on horseback. Whenever Marieke takes a stroll around the castle, her minder seems to pop up at the most unexpected moments, preventing her from going anywhere near the castle gate. Occasionally she sees Ingeborg, who is eager to practice her English, and Marieke is keen to teach her. After all, the more Ingeborg understands, the better her chances of getting out. So far, Ingeborg hasn't been able to tell her where they are, or even what time they're supposed to be in. Marieke hesitates to ask about that strange word, her tight stomach telling her that she doesn't really want to know the answer.

One day the sky seems almost blue, the clouds thin veils clinging on to each other's wispy hands. Marieke walks up to the battlements, convinced the fjord-like channel will be expectedly lovely in this light. She is right. The blue water is more vibrant than ever and she smiles, letting the soft breeze float across her face. Idly, she looks around, her eyes following the blue of the water. Then she narrows her eyes, adjusting her glasses. Something is coming up the fjord. A boat. It's white, and the more she stares, the more she is convinced it is a large ship. A modern ship, not a Viking longboat. She blinks, opens her eyes as wide as possible. It's a modern ship, like a cruise ship. She can feel her legs shaking with excitement. A ship, a modern ship, and it's coming closer! Should she try to get out, and run down the track to the beach? Should she get her red-brown cloak, and wave it? The boat glides irritatingly slowly across the blue water, coming closer nonetheless. Marieke's heart is beating as if she has been running on the treadmill at home, and her hands are clenched together.

The next thing she knows, Harald and her minder are running

along the battlement, calling out something to her in impatient voices. She gives an angry gasp and turns her back on them. She hasn't seen or heard them, she isn't going to let them take away her one chance of getting away from this hateful place. She looks back at the white ship, which she can tell by now is definitely a cruise ship, fear making her heart race this time. She needs to contact them, they simply have to spot her, help her, rescue her! Now!

Chapter 11

Within seconds the two men have reached her, and hard hands grab her, dragging her towards the battlement stairs. Marieke struggles as hard as she can, feeling her very survival depends on being spotted by the ship, digging her heels in, trying to grab at the stone battlements...all to no avail. Harald reached her first, something she is fleetingly grateful for, as the other man looks more than ready to drag her along by her hair. "No, no!" she gasps, frantically twisting her neck to look at the fjord, still and unrippled, unaware of her turmoil so far above. The cruise ship full of people unaware of her very existence. If only she could signal, make them aware, call out for help. Without too much effort Harald gets her out of sight of the cruise ship, the fjord, the battlements. Only when they get to the apartments does she stop fighting.

Not that Marieke walks along, but she has simply run out of breath and energy to fight, gasping for air, fury making her feel sick. She is pretty sure she hit Harald hard a few times, only because her hands feel bruised, which is the tiny bit of satisfaction she has. When they get to her room, he pushes her in, then slips out of the room quickly, shutting the door before she can steady herself enough to rush at the door. She can hear him say something, her minder answers, then receding footsteps. Marieke is desperate and angry, as well as confused. What is the cruise ship doing in the fjord? She can't think about that now, she needs to get out. When she tries to open the door, she finds the handle won't turn. Ah, so the Sulky one is holding the handle, is he? She presses her lips together, and tries and tries again, banging on the door at the same time, demanding he lets her out, or else.

It seems Sulky has an 'or else' in mind as well, for suddenly the door flings open, just when she wants to kick it, and he appears, his face red, eyes narrowed at her. She staggers because of the loss of target, and he closes in swiftly, punching and pummelling her, kneeing her, carefully avoiding her face. Marieke cries out, but the wind is knocked out of her, silencing her, leaving her merely gasping for breath. She tries to protect herself as much as possible, half turning away from him. Another hard punch, sending her flying, Marieke trips over her own feet, her head hitting the flagstone floor with an oddly loud thud, her glasses sliding off her nose. When the blackness fades, she can see his sulky face, his three faces even, or is it two? Maybe four. She closes her eyes, the world spinning too fast for comfort. For a tiny second, she feels satisfied with the shocked look on his face.

When she opens her eyes again, she is alone. For a moment she stares at the flagstones near her face, wondering what she is doing on the floor. She gasps. The ship. Harald and her minder. The world no longer spins, and Marieke reaches out, her fingers curling round her glasses. She feels them carefully. Nothing seems broken, and she releases her breath. Her shaking hands struggle with her glasses, but she is finally ready to move. The world punishes her instantly by spinning faster than ever, not just one way either. She closes her eyes quickly, leaning her head on the cold floor. Her head throbs and each inner knock stimulates her stomach to throb along. After a few minutes, when she is quite sure that things have stabilised as much as they're going to, Marieke slowly moves along the floor, keeping her eyes shut. Her ears make a wild whooshing sound, her head hammers, and she concentrates hard on calm, even breathing, hoping her stomach will merely quiver, not rebel outright. She has to stop every two inches, breathing out in soft whimpers.

At last, Marieke makes it to her bed and hesitates. Should she get on? She peeks through her eye lashes, the light hitting her immediately. She tries to take a few deeper breaths, then pulls herself up onto the bed, crying out in pain as her ribs bump the soft mattress. Her arms won't support her and for a few seconds she considers staying on the floor, but she knows she'll regret that. Draped on the edge of the bed, she swallows down on sharpness in her throat, her half-formed thoughts alternating between prayers, curses aimed at her sulky minder, more prayers for forgiveness of evil thoughts, panic over losing the cruise ship and the escape it represents. Inch by inch she drags herself further onto the bed. Once she lies down, Marieke groans, wanting to cry, but too sore to do so. Her one arm shakes and protests, but she manages to touch her head where it collided with the flagstones. There is a huge lump, but it doesn't feel wet or sticky. She rubs her fingers along the lump a few times, then squints at her hand. No blood. Good, that's something at least.

Marieke stays still, covering her eyes with the sheet to try and darken the room. Every time she moves, the sickness is stronger.

She dozes, unable to think straight, wondering if the cruise ship is part of the weird fantasy she seems to have landed in. The queasiness makes her believe she is still on a rocking ferry, and the Vikings, fjords and Cruise ships are a dream. A soft knock brings her back to the surface, and she tries to look, but the light is too strong. Footsteps come closer, a gasp, and when Marieke tries to look again, Gunilla's face is near hers, the usual smile replaced with a look of horror. Marieke swallows the sharp taste in her throat down and makes her hand touch the lump again. Gunilla's fingers join hers, "Oh, Marieke!" Gunilla notices the way her arm moves and carefully moves her sleeves up. Another "Oh!" Marieke tries to smile but is doesn't work. The light is more bearable though, and she looks at Gunilla who seems to turn into a two-headed beauty every few heartbeats.

Gunilla says something, but Marieke has no idea. The woman bites her lip, then lights up. She taps her arm, her head, then shrugs and flaps her hands around her body. Marieke understands and points to her ribs. Gunilla takes hold of Marieke's dress, raising her eyebrows. Marieke almost nods, but the first movement towards doing so brings her four Gunillas. Gunilla raises the dress, and gasps when she sees Marieke's ribs. When she looks at Marieke again, she looks nothing like the giggling friend Marieke has got to know. "Harald?" she asks, and Marieke breathes out a soft 'nei'. Gunilla frowns and says another name. Marieke tries to pull the most sulky face she can, a shaking hand drawing the thick eyebrows, floppy moustache and long hair. Gunilla nods, her face red, eyes darker grey than the North Sea during a Northwester.

Gunilla pulls the sheet back over Marieke's eyes, touches her shoulder lightly, but not lightly enough as Marieke takes a sharp breath. Then Gunilla is gone. Marieke thinks she can hear her disappearing footsteps, then realises it's the hammering in her head making the clonking noise. Tears roll down, but her ribs ache too much to sob. What if she has broken her ribs? She's quite sure she has a concussion, but what if it's a really serious one? Do they have a Viking hospital? Her head aches, she just wants…wants whatever will make it better. She thinks of her phone, then remembers there's no signal. New tears roll, burning her eyes, making the nausea worse, her head drumming enthusiastically along with each breath. "In through the nose, out through the mouth," she whispers at herself, needing to hear a voice she can understand.

Minutes stagger by. Over the throbbing, she can hear footsteps. Self-pity and loneliness have been growing steadily, pressing her down like a weighted blanket. Now somebody is coming, someone has thought of her. The rough voice growling at her is like an unexpected cold shower, making her gasp, then cry out in pain. It is Sulky, towering over her, his eyes narrow, arms crossed, lips curled in a sneer. He leans over her, repeating his words. She closes her eyes with a groan, but Sulky grabs her arm, making her cry out, then throw up. The last thing Marieke notices before the blackness carries her off is two-fold: she was sick all over his leather boots, and Erika and Gunilla are at the door, their eyes and faces scaring even Sulky.

Chapter 12

When the darkness recedes, Marieke is alone. The castle is quiet as always, and she can tell from her tiny slit window that it's afternoon. The thought that she can tell the time of day from her window depresses her somehow. It shows her that she has been here too long. As she can't move her head without feeling sick, she knows she will be here a bit longer. Unless Harald lets her go, taking her back to wherever she should be, Dover or Dunkirk. She sighs, then half coughs and whimpers with the pain. Her ribs really hurt. How does she check if they're broken? And would it make a difference? The idea of being pulled onto a horse again for the ride back to the ferry doesn't make her feel better at all.

Soft footsteps approach again, and Marieke squints at the door. It is Erika, holding a glass of water and something to eat. It's the flatbread like she had the first day. Erika smiles at her, her eyes worried. Very slowly and carefully she helps Marieke to sit up a little, then holds the glass to her mouth. Marieke fights down the nausea, knowing she needs to eat and drink, her breath coming in gasps. Marieke's hands shake, her arms stiff and painful, unwilling to cooperate. She is glad to nibble the bread, as she felt hungry as well as queasy, knowing the food will help her stomach to settle.

Marieke is relieved to lie down again, giving Erika a watery smile. Erika touches her shoulder with her fingertips, smiles, and quietly leaves her room, shutting the door gently. Marieke closes her eyes, exhausted, her body shivering with shock. Soon she drifts off to sleep, plagued by dreams of cruise ships filled with Vikings wearing dinner jackets, punching people to the ground, and drinking curried coffee.

When she wakes up in the morning, she finds her whole body stiff. Nevertheless, she feels better, although moving her head the slightest bit brings back queasiness with great enthusiasm. She groans, trying to position herself on the bed in a more comfortable way, although the pain it takes makes her wonder if it's worth it. The door opens, and Gunilla appears with food and some water. It's the usual porridge, and Marieke shudders then spots the quantities of honey. She hadn't realised they had all noticed how much honey she put on her porridge. She can feel her face warm up, but smiles at Gunilla. The woman helps her to sit up, and Marieke grinds her teeth to stop herself from crying out. She is out of breath by the time she sits up enough to eat.

Porridge makes her gag a little, but the cold water is refreshing. Gunilla touches the lump on her head very gently, her eyes dark, lips pressed together. She says, "Sven" and shakes her head, looking angry. Marieke assumes Sven is Sulky, but somehow having a name feels wrong. She doesn't want to think of him as Sven. Simply Sulky will do. Her heart beats faster just thinking of him. The anger drums away inside her, making breathing hard. She is relieved when she's alone again, closing her eyes against the morning light. Images of Sulky's mean face drift past her, as well as the shocked look after she fell.

She pushes that one away. Thinking of him having to clean his boots makes her smile, her fists clenched. Soon she drifts off to sleep again, her pillow wet with tears.

The next few days pass in peace, quiet and boredom. Marieke is determined to rest well and refuses to leave her room. There is no way she will confront everyone until her head is better. She will need her wits and energy back before seeing Sulky and the other grumps. By the end of the week, she feels well enough to venture out. She wakes up quite early and decides to wash her hair. The huge lump is slightly less huge, but still very tender. Rinsing the soap out of her hair is complex, but she is satisfied in the end. She gentle dries it, then rakes it with her fingers, sitting on her bed, her arms stiff and trembling a little. Patience is a virtue, she tells herself, struggling with each strand of hair. She feels better though, putting a tiny bit of coconut oil on her face, wondering how long it will take for her skin to feel smooth and radiant again after an oil-free week. She puts on one of her Viking dresses with stripes as well as embroidery. By the time she is ready for breakfast, she is exhausted but glad to feel more human.

She walks slowly to the dining room, her head feeling heavy, and her legs shaking a little with the effort. No chance of running away this night, clearly. When she walks into the room there is a surprised gasp, and Gunilla and Erika beam at her. Hillevi glares at her, her eyes travelling up and down, the corners of her mouth turned even further down than usual. Harald seems mildly less grumpy, you would almost think he was pleased to see her. She makes sure to avoid looking at Sulky. The servant holds the carafe with the herby fermented drink over her glass, then hesitates, and points at it, then at the door and says, "Vatn," looking at her for confirmation. Marieke nods and repeats the word for water. She doesn't think the drink has that much alcohol, but still… She is pleased that the servant knows she prefers water, at the same time feeling irritated by it. It's another sign that she has been here way too long. If they think she's going to be grateful and happy to stay, they're mistaken. She is staying, because there is no other option at the moment.

After breakfast she drifts towards the door, seemingly relaxed, her hands cold and clammy. Before she knows it she is back on the battlements, her legs shaking now. Her eyes squint against the morning sun shining on the fjord, but there is no cruise ship. Was there one before? Maybe the knock on her head confused her. After all, how does a modern cruise ship fit in? There is the ferry, of course, and her car. At least there was. She has no idea where her little red tin box is now. Are these Vikings squatters, like a hippy commune that has taken over and renovated an old castle? She is sure it's not a dream, but how did she end up in this world? Is it even the same world? Her head starts to hurt trying to figure it out, and even though leaning on the battlements helps her to catch her breath, she can feel the effects of being on her feet this long.

Her weakness worries her. She needs to get out of here, and Marieke is still convinced that freedom lies somewhere near the fjord. After all, that is where the madness truly began. She has a hard job getting from the battlements to the apartments, let alone hike to the fjord! She will need to regain strength, and quickly. If this is some northern, Viking-type country, the summer will bring very long daylight hours. She needs darkness to get out. By the time she has joined Gunilla and Erika, Marieke almost feels like kissing her chair. She is sweating as if she has been on the treadmill listening to a couple of podcasts, rather than simply walk through a castle. Her arms are still a little sore, but soon Marieke is working away.

She has struggled with this point, and with her head drumming away after the walk, she struggles anew. As the enemy has kidnapped her, and are still keeping her against her will, should she do all she can to sabotage them? Should she somehow make the thread so fragile that it becomes useless (given she could figure out how to do this in the first place), should she point blank refuse to leave her room? She could simply meditate and pray, using her time in a godly way. Or should she actually pull her weight? The first day she had done the work simply to be with Gunilla and Erika, because they had been kind, and because she had no idea what to do otherwise. She thought about it. After all, these people might all be fakes, like actors or hippies. Or just a figment of her imagination. On the other hand, Marieke feels that like Daniel she should be a blessing where ever she is and bring prosperity to the place. Not that spinning wool is going to bring in bags of money, but it is something.

So she does her best and tries to show her willingness, hoping those around her will think her a testimony of…of…well, that's the awkward thing. She doesn't speak the language, so she can't share her faith or point out that the only reason she is prepared to ruin her fingernails and fingertips is to show them a better Way. Do Vikings even know the word 'blessing', as they seemed happy to take her along? Didn't Vikings plunder and loot? Also, given the anger, hatred and turmoil inside her, isn't it being a hypocrite? Should she show her true colours? Maybe she ought to pray more, and trust God with the outcome. Aren't all trouble in our life sent to test us, to bring us closer to God? Should she see it more as a blessing and a chance to grow in grace? When Marieke thinks of Sulky pushing her, of Harald dragging her off the battlements, and keeping her here, she feels her entire body tighten up with resentment. It might not be very Christian, but surely God knows that she's merely human? Maybe she should simply spin the wool, smile and stay out of bright sunlight, as her paracetamols aren't going to cope with this growing headache. She thinks fondly back to one of the sales representatives who loved philosophising, and how she had laughed at him, called him the Mad Professor. Now she's growing a shocking headache, debating the pros and cons of blessing fake people. Or are they fake?

Chapter 13

Marieke is determined to get well and strong as soon as possible. She decides to do a quick bodyweight workout in her room every morning and evening, just to get her strength back. She also takes a walk round the castle twice a day. Up and down the battlements, across the courtyard. Most days Sulky pops up several times, and she feels great satisfaction in the fact that his limp is definitely more pronounced by the time they get back to the apartment. Serves him right. Not a very Christian attitude, of course, so she tries to tell herself that she is doing him a favour by getting him in better shape as well.

She notices the days are getting longer, especially on sunny days, and feels a tightening sensation in her stomach. She needs to get out, as the walk to the fjord will take a long time, and she'll be seen in the light of the morning. She will need to wait till dark to get out of the castle, and wants to be at the fjord before dawn. She passes the stables on her walks, trying to stay away as far as possible from the open doors where the horse smells and noises come from. For a while she thought of stealing a horse, jump on its back, and gallop out of the gate across the drawbridge, and down to the fjord, her hair streaming behind her. Her tight curls never 'stream' behind her, not even in a gale and the idea of going into the stable and grabbing a horse by its mane makes her feel physically sick. Of course, in books, a woman can pray for strength, then find her fears miraculously disappeared under the onslaught of Bible verses. The transformed character then goes on to defeat all enemies, her old fears conquered forever.

Marieke tries praying over the stable entrance, but the smells and sounds still have the same effect on her. She's obviously doing something wrong, for her prayer to overcome her fear of horses hasn't had the wished-for effect. Faith might move mountains but clearly doesn't work on horses. Not for her, anyway. Maybe it's to do with her prayers against the Viking bunch? Or maybe she should step out in faith, and grab a horse before the fear leaves her? Marieke isn't prepared to try it, and deep down she knows she ought to feel guilty about her anger against Sulky. On the other hand, he hasn't done anything to endear himself to her. The least he could have done was apologise to her. Instead, he glares at her whenever he sees her, and his sulky face goes dark every time he spots her. Once, she caught him looking at his boots as soon as he saw her. That brought a giggle; ah, so he is angry with her for throwing up over his precious boots! Well, he should have known better than grabbing her.

Marieke is looking forward to washing day, the one day the entire castle has a bath. She had been pleasantly surprised the first time, and now counts the days till the next round. She will never take showers for granted again, or baths with good smelling bath stuff. The woman helping her with her bath keeps exclaiming over her hair, even feeling it. Marieke had grinned the first time it happened, feeling embarrassed at the same time.

The woman had been so amazed and enthusiastic about it, that she couldn't feel cross with her. Every time she turned and saw Marieke's hair she would shake her head and tut, her face sad as she mutters that word again. Traelinna. Marieke feels her face glowing, and it's not because of the coarse soap or hot water. At least she hasn't felt her skin, despite giving Marieke's arms some serious stares.

That evening she goes for her usual stroll along the battlements. The weather has been grey all day, and a few times a light drizzle has drifted down over the castle, no sign of the fjord. The steps are a little slippery because of the wetness, but at least the rain has stopped. Marieke feels tired; it must be to do with the weather, she thinks, and she looks forward to dinner time. Having only two meals a day works out alright, but does make her ravenous by the time dinner is served. She is looking forward to an early night as well. Her hair is finally dry, and she needs to rub some coconut oil in it, otherwise, the curls will get too brittle and lack lustre. She bites her lip, her oil is almost gone. She wonders if the kitchen has different types of oils and whether any of them would work in her hair. The idea of rubbing lard all over her hair makes her shudder.

A few times, Marieke feels somebody is walking just behind her. She glances round but sees no one there. Once when she looks round, Sulky is just coming up the stairs behind her, his face looking more threatening than the rain clouds overhead. She glares back, and moves a little faster, down some steps, along another part of the castle where she can see some of the men working on something. She hesitates, should she go and look, pretending to be interested? Just being with other people will make her feel safer. Then she spots Leer, her old friend from the ferry, and she promptly changes course. Sulky might be a nuisance, but Leer…she feels cold remembering his looks on the ferry. Harald had stopped him that time, but walking straight up to him might be a bad move.

Instead, she veers off towards the kitchen, with its wonderful cooking smells. The roasting meat smell reminds her of summer barbecues, her dad burning the sausages somehow, no matter how much they watched him. Tears sting, she wants to be home, wants to eat chocolate sprinkles on soft white bread, wants a huge slice of Dutch 'taart', several layers of super soft cake, held together by sweet cream, bits of fruit and chocolate on top. She wants to ride her bike, go shopping, have coffee with friends on a terrace, watching the world go by. She wants, she needs to get out of this weird world. The kitchen is hot, and she hesitates. She doesn't know how to ask for oil! Suddenly Ingeborg appears next to her, looking a little surprised. Marieke smiles, relief making her smile huge. "Hi! I was looking for oil. Do they use oil in cooking?" Ingeborg hesitates, her mind flicking through her internal dictionary.

"Oll?" Marieke nods, not bothering to correct, and her eyes wander round the kitchen. She sees a frying pan with a long handle and points to it.

"Oil, to stop food from sticking on. Looks a bit like water, but is fat." Ingeborg nods and beckons her to come along. To Marieke's relief, she shows her a few glass bottles, with what looks like oil. But what kind of oil? "What is the oil made of?" Ingeborg purses her lips then tells her to wait and soon returns with a few walnuts. Marieke heaves a sigh of relief. Walnut oil would be perfect. Coconut oil is her preferred oil of course, but walnut oil is better than sunflower or anything else that will make her smell like her mum's kitchen after her dad finished cooking 'oliebollen' on New Year's Eve. One of the kitchen maids comes with a small dish and hands it to Marieke. She looks so curious, that once Marieke has poured some into the dish, she dips her fingers in, then rubs the oil on her springy hair. "My hair gets very dry, then breaks easily," she tells Ingeborg, who passes on this bit of information to the girl. The girl's eyes had opened wide when Marieke rubbed the oil in her hair, now she nods. Gingerly she touches one of the strands, then nods again, and says something to Ingeborg.

"Ee hair, is dry, yes?" Ingeborg says, and Marieke nods. The girls now study the oiled strand, and Ingeborg agrees, "Is better. No dry." Marieke smiles at them, and thanks the girl for the dish and the oil. Ingeborg proudly translates, the girl's eyes showing her admiration for her fellow servant. For a moment Marieke enjoys the moment. It just feels so normal, hanging out with other girls, talking hair. There is nothing normal about her life just now, though, and although these girls are friendly, they're servants. She isn't, not really, although she still isn't sure why Harald brought her here. He isn't going to pay for her upkeep forever, is he? He isn't looking after her out of the goodness of his heart either. He brought her here for a reason, and Marieke is pretty sure that she won't be impressed with his reason. She still remembers Hillevi's reaction that first evening when Marieke appeared at the dinner table. No, there is something fishy about the whole thing. For now, she's happy she has oil and some kind women around her. She's doing her best to count her blessings.

Walnut oil still smells a little foodie, but Marieke sighs with relief when her hair is done that evening, leaving a tiny scraping of coconut oil for her face. Maybe they have some essential oils, she wonders. She could mix that into the walnut oil, and that would make her smell less like fried chicken. It's bad enough her arms, legs and hands smelling of nuts, but her face...

Chapter 14

The weather stays grey for several days, with the occasional shower. Marieke feels it pulling her down, longing for the sun to come out. Every time she goes for a stroll around the battlements she stares through the greyness, hoping to see the fjord, hoping to catch sight of another cruise ship. She needs to get out. The way Harald and Hillevi look at her makes her uncomfortable. Something is brewing, she can feel it. Of course, she might be paranoid, but they won't have brought her to this castle for no reason at all. They are not keeping her, feeding her, clothing her for the bit of spinning she does, are they? No, she is sure she caught Harald's look last night, the way he and Sulky talked quietly, looking at her. She overheard that word again. Traelinna. She needs to ask Ingeborg.

She shivers. Marieke pulls the woollen cloak tighter around herself, the door to the apartments closing behind her. Her coat got damp this morning, so the Viking cloak will need to do. It's obvious why somebody invented a coat with sleeves and a zip, she thinks, rearranging the cloak with a quick arm movement. You'd need a total absence of wind for starters. The castle is quiet, apart from a metallic banging from the smithy. The fire gives off a warm, inviting glow, and Marieke can see some of the guys hanging around the door. She can't blame them. Shivering, she walks across the courtyard towards the steps, not far from the large gate leading to the drawbridge, the only way out. She has to stay fit; the trek to the fjord won't be easy.

Once on the battlements, the wind feels damp, laced with specks of rain. She looks towards where she knows the fjord is, where freedom starts. No sign of water at all, apart from the occasional drop landing on her face to substitute tears sprung into her eyes from disappointment. She is glad to dry her face every now and again, as crying over mist is not an option. Her time will come, she has to believe that. Abruptly, she turns her back on the fjord, physically as well as mentally, and decides to walk around the entire battlements, past the round tower, back to where she started, as the exercise will do her good, and she needs to keep up her fitness. She misses her morning runs, something she would never dare to admit out loud.

Walking around the corner, Marieke is sure she can hear someone else on the battlements. There are guards on each side, but she can see the one in front of her, and she is sure the noise comes from behind her, but when she looks around there is nobody there. It might be Sulky, of course, as he tends to still follow her around. For a moment she wonders what would happen if she hopped over the battlement, into the moat down below, and ran off. The guards at the drawbridge would be waiting for her to clamber from the moat, so she gives up on that idea. When she nears the round tower, she looks over her shoulder again, uneasiness swirling in the air with the drizzle.

The round tower overshadows the battlement, the building creating a tunnel with dark corners, small nooks filled with birds nests and dust. A few steps into the tunnel and Marieke spins round. The noise behind her no longer a hint of a person's presence. It is Sulky, looking at her with his grumpy face twisted, a bright gleam in his eyes. He almost looks pleased with life, her life, she realises. With a quick step, he closes the gap and grabs her wrist. Marieke gasps, and before he steadies his grip, she has wrenched her wrist free, thankful that the self-defence course in secondary school finally does pay off. She spins round, and runs off further into the tunnel, frantically looking ahead to the end of the round tower, and hopefully the next guard. All is dark, and she can hear Sulky gaining on her. A solid figure looms up suddenly, but Marieke's half cry of relief breaks off. It is Leer, looking more leery than ever at seeing the momentary look of pleasure on her face. The fact that relief turns to horror within seconds seems to brighten his unpleasant face even more.

Seeing Sulky turn up behind Marieke takes his smile right off his face, however. He glares at Sulky, who has grabbed Marieke again, pulling her back towards himself. Marieke struggles and fights, then Leer steps forward, and grabs her other arm, growling something at Sulky. Sulky answers back, his face in an angry snarl, lips curled back like a wild animal, pointing at Marieke and tugging at her. Leer smirks, pulls Marieke away from Sulky, nodding at her and saying something in a jeering voice, his lips twisted in an ugly grin. Sulky's face goes a dark red, and he steps closer to Leer, his eyebrows touching each other over murderous eyes. They're fighting over her, and Marieke can feel sweat running down the back of her linen dress. Desperation makes her fight harder, her breath coming in wild gasps. She has to get away from these two, and soon! Sulky tries to pull her closer, but Leer pulls her back with a cruel jerk. Marieke cries out in pain, but neither man looks at her. Suddenly, Leer produces a knife. For a split second Sulky lets go, and she twists away. He merely changes hands though, his right hand holding a dagger as well. Marieke's legs suddenly feel jellified. Two angry guys with knives and she is stuck in the middle. She doesn't want to be the first prize, fought over by the winner, and she doesn't want to end up as collateral damage either.

She cries out feebly for the guard. Where are guardsmen when you need them? Before she has finished the first syllable, both men shake her so roughly, that no more words can come out. At least they agreed on that one. With Marieke sorted out, they concentrate on each other again. Leer suddenly stabs towards Sulky, who merely moves out of the way a little, returning with his own slashing movement. Marieke dimly realises that this is where her chances lie. Whenever they stab or fight, she has that split-second moment of distraction. The stabbings follow each other more quickly, and Marieke feels her fear growing along with the men's anger and frustration. Leer stabs again, using the dagger as a short sword, the thrust lower than Marieke thought would count as fair. Sulky reacts by aiming a wild slash at Leer's red hot face, but the knife never comes close to Leer's long hair and carefully kempt moustache. With one flick of his arm, he has manoeuvred Marieke in the path of Sulk's dagger.

She feels the prick of the dagger tip on her arm, the slicing of fabric, then the hot searing pain on her cheek. Marieke screams in pain and horror, her hand suddenly free to cover her face, feeling the wetness instantly. Sulky looks shocked, with the same wide-open eyes as he had when she hit the ground in her room. Leer takes his chance, and his dagger flashes in the dim light and Sulky finds himself fighting for his own skin. Marieke is free, both men engrossed in their battle. Holding her face, she staggers through the tunnel, sobbing, her face wet with blood and tears. "I hate you, I hate you, I hope Leer will get you. I hope you will both get each other…" She has no idea how bad the cut is, whether it's a simple scratch or a proper cut. The fact it's bleeding doesn't say too much, as facial cuts do bleed. It hurts though, it really, really hurts, and she knows it can't be a mere scratch. What is she going to do?

Stumbling across the courtyard of the castle, she carries on sobbing, "No guard helped, nobody even asked, nobody is even here, they don't care if I was raped, killed or cut up, but as soon as I try to get out they're all there to stop me. I hate them, I hate them all, I wished some other tribe would come and flatten the lot, I hope Leer gets Sulky properly!" Once inside, in the light of the smoky torches, she has a quick look at her hand. Seeing her hand and wrist drenched in blood makes her gasp in horror, her sobbing way more frantic now. What if she bleeds to death? How long does it take for a person to bleed to death?

Chapter 15

Edging on the hysterical, Marieke staggers into her room, straight to the round basin. She quickly rinses her hand in the cold water left in the basin, then pours more water onto the thin flannel type cloth. Carefully she dabs it at her face, the water stinging the cut. Or is it the salt from her tears? Through blurry eyes, she can see the water in the basin turning a worrying red. Marieke keeps telling herself it only looks like that because of the water, it always looks worse than it is; it's simply because it's a cut on her face… She hears running footsteps, and turns to the door, her glasses steamed up. Erika and Gunilla appear, their faces worried. When they see her face, they both cry out in shock, adding to Marieke's fears. Erika clamps her hand over her mouth as if regretting her outburst. They rush to her side, and Erika takes the wet cloth from Marieke.

Gunilla turns her round so they can see the cut on her face, and Erika dabs gently at the cut. Marieke simply sobs, her main thought being that she will have a scar on her face for life. After a while Erika leans back a little, signifying that this is as good as it's going to get. Within a few seconds, she leans forward again, dabbing the fresh blood away. Marieke points to her handbag, then slowly walks over to it, Erika following her, hovering with the cloth. Marieke digs through her handbag and brings out the box with Steristrips. One summer she cut herself on the beach, and since then she carries a pack of Steristrips, 'just in case'. She is glad to have them now and thinks triumphantly about all the times people questioned her about the need to carry 'all that stuff' in her handbag.

She takes her tiny hand mirror out as well, and with shaking hands manages to open the pack. She peels the first strip off, then looks in the mirror, Erika obligingly drying the wound again. Marieke gives a loud gasp when she sees the cut. It's even worse than she thought! Will Steristrips even do it? What if the cut gets infected? With difficulty, she places the first strip over the top end of the cut, not that far from her eye. She forces her mind to stay away from all the 'what ifs' that swirl around inside her head. "Focus," she whispers to herself with a sob, needing to hear a voice she understands, rather than the soft, worried conversation between Erika and Gunilla, tuning out the word 'traelinna'.

The two women are amazed at the little white strip that not only stays on but actually keeps the wound closed tightly at the same time. Once Marieke has put the second strip on, Erika hands the red cloth to Gunilla, and takes the pack of Steristrips from Marieke's shaking hands. Carefully she peels the next strip off and places it on Marieke's cut. Both are now leaning right into her face, eyes wide open, enthralled by this modern miracle. Marieke does her best to stop crying, feeling a bit embarrassed to do so with the two women that close by. Watching the cut turning into a train track with white sleepers makes her more furious with each strip. How dare they do this to her? How dare they attack her in the first place, then fight over her, and deform her for life. Well, deform might be a bit of a strong word, but scar her. Scar her for life, that is sure.

Marieke has seen people whose scars grew and grew; Keloid Scars, and she knows that there is a chance this will happen to her. What if the scar stays pink, like a glow in the dark strip on her face? What if it becomes a thick, pink track across her face? Will she need plastic surgery to sort it out? Will the NHS even cover it, and when? Erika looks at her, slightly puzzled. She must have felt the tension and anger in Marieke's jaw. She points at the cut and asks something. Marieke tries to remember Sulky's name and ends up pulling a grumpy face, and making a limping motion whilst still sitting down. "Sven," cry Gunilla and Erika at the same time. Marieke nods, satisfied, yes, Sven. And Leer, but how does she explain that one? She starts acting out the fight, too tired to get off the floor all of a sudden. Both women look completely lost, and Marieke almost giggles. She is hopeless at charades, even with parties, nobody wants her on their team!

She indicates two people and makes stabbing movements. The women nod. She indicates Leer's long hair (most of the guys seem to have shoulder length hair), his moustache (she can't remember seeing any of the guys without one), and does the looking up and down. That more or less describes every guy in the castle as well, she sighs. Even the large black guy she saw the other day, although he had curled his lips in disdain once he reached her face, and turned away. Her heart had sunk.

Just when she is about to give up, Ingeborg suddenly appears at the door. The three women sat on the floor stare at her. Ingeborg looks upset, but when she sees Marieke's face she gives a small cry, smothering the rest with both her hands over

73

her mouth. Marieke can feel new tears warm up, wondering if people will be reacting to her like this for the rest of her life. A tiny part whispers that she might be overreacting, but she pushes that thought away. If these Viking women react like that when seeing blood and wounds, well, it must be bad. Ingeborg steps into the room, after a quick look over her shoulder down the corridor. She closes the door and drops down near the other three. She looks at Erika and Gunilla and says something in an urgent, dramatic whisper. The only word she understands is 'Holmgang'. The word is repeated in horror by Gunilla, as both women look at her with wide eyes, and Erika frowns. They both turn back to Ingeborg, almost daring her to admit she'd exaggerated.

Ingeborg turns to Marieke, ignoring the hard stares from the others. "Ee go," she says urgently. Go? Kidding right, Marieke has wanted to go for ages, but it's not as easy as it sounds, especially with nobody helping her. "Ee go, now," Ingeborg continues. "Sven and Orm, have Holmgang. Kill, then ee," and she links her fingers together, waving them towards Marieke, "Ee trälinna. Slav. Slav Womans." Marieke makes her mind catch up on this news. She assumes Orm is Leer, he and Sulky have Holmgang whatever that is, but it seems to involve killing, then it links her up. Hang on, does she mean they will fight over her like a duel, and she gets to marry the one that doesn't get killed? And that word, trälinna, means slave? Like a slave woman? She asks Ingeborg.

"You mean they will fight, and then I get married off to the winner? And I'm a slave?" she looks at Ingeborg, and has to ask again, her charades skills developing quickly. In the end, Ingeborg nods, "Yes, ee marry. Sven or Orm, yes. You Slav, trälinna." Marieke shudders. Ingeborg is right, she needs to get out. "Ee go. When dark," Ingeborg says, then says something to the other woman, who both nod, whilst stealing glances at the door. "This time dark, after food, when slepping." Ingeborg says, and Gunilla and Erika nod, agreeing with Ingeborg, even though they don't understand the words. Escape? Tonight? Marieke feels dizzy with excitement and this evening's shock. She's getting out. Tonight! And her friends have finally agreed to help her get away. Better late than never, she supposes, but her resentment fades away in the face of her joy.

Chapter 16

Marieke feels a shiver of apprehension. She has no idea how to travel through the dark forest in the middle of the night, and the castle suddenly feels like a safe haven. A spark of hope has ignited though, and she turns her attention back to her friends. She understands from Ingeborg that it will be late at night, but how and when? The four women sit down, and Marieke pulls a notebook and pen from her bag. The other three reach over and touch the paper, staring at the pen. Marieke bites her lip, trying to imagine what it's like to see pen and paper for the first time, but now is not the moment for a stationary tour. She sketches the castle outline, the gate, the moat. She taps the paper pointing out what each thing is. She's better at Picture-It than charades. Ingeborg repeats the words, and they all nod.

The three Viking women lean over the paper, and in the end, Erika draws wide circles around the castle with her finger and says a word. "Where go?" Ingeborg translates, and Marieke nods, draws the fjord, with little waves. They all nod again, making her smile. Then Erika taps the paper left of the gate and says something to Ingeborg. "Ee out," she translates, "water, walk, yes?" Marieke nods along. Yes, through the moat, then follow the road down to the fjord. Erika reaches and carefully takes the pen. She looks doubtful but puts the tip on the paper, delighted to see the line appear. She points, draws, gestures towards Ingeborg and Gunilla, more drawing, until all four lean back with a satisfied sigh. Marieke beams, although she tries to temper her smile. It feels a bit awkward to show these three women how enormously relieved she will be to get away from them.

She feels indebted to them, they have been kind and helpful, and now they're risking an awful lot to get her out. Will there be repercussions for them? They have to make sure that it looks like she got out all by herself. The three leave as the dinner signal sounds. Marieke takes another look in her tiny hand mirror, trying to wipe blood spatters off the cover. There is blood everywhere, she realises as she struggles into a clean dress. On the floor tiles, the door, the wash basin, everywhere. She hesitates, but her growling stomach decides that dinner comes first. She thinks about cleaning up afterwards. It depends on who will have to do it if she doesn't do it. Part of her sees it as retribution for wounding her, keeping her prisoner all this time. She doesn't like the idea of her three friends having to do it, though.

She walks into the dining room, and Hillevi gasps out loud. Thanks, Marieke thinks bitterly, and her mood freezes over even more as Harald glares at her cut, as if he thinks she has done it on purpose. Sulky smirks, but pulls his standard glum face when he meets Harald's furious eyes. Harald leans over to him and says something, making Sulky blush and practice drilling holes in his plate with his looks. Did Harald tell him off for damaging merchandise? She can't imagine Harald feeling sorry for her just because she got a cut. No, he wouldn't tell

Sulky off if it was just for her sake only. Well, if she's nowhere to be found tomorrow, Sulky might be in even more trouble. She hardly tastes her dinner, glad about the water, but chewing isn't working out so well. As soon as she tries, tears sting her eye, and she keeps her head down. Her cheek throbs, and for a moment she panics. Did the cut go right through? Should she have checked the inside of her mouth? Her tongue feels odd with fear, but gingerly she feels with the tip of her tongue, soon convinced that the inside of her mouth is still intact.

When dinner is finished, Harald turns to Sulky. Hillevi is listening in, so Marieke takes this opportunity to slide her knife up her sleeve. She has been wanting to do this for ages, but an opportunity never seems to present itself. This time, she is more determined. She needs the idea that she has a weapon. She leaves the dining room, worried someone will see her knife is missing, but Gunilla and Erika have started to stack plates and cutlery. She smiles to herself when the door shuts behind her. She will miss those two, as well as Ingeborg. It's the guys, Sulky, Leer, Harald... How dare they bring her here, now she's going home damaged. Home... she sighs with happiness and walks that little bit faster to her room. Ingeborg is cleaning the tiles. She looks up with a smile, and soon Marieke is helping her to put things straight in her room. The dress is covered in blood, as well as ripped at the shoulder. When Ingeborg is finished, they look at Marieke's clothes together. What should she wear? Something dark, preferably. Her dresses are rather light though, and Ingeborg walks off with the dirty wash basin. When she returns, she has a dark blue dress, reminding Marieke of Amish films. Minus the head covering, she grins to herself, wondering how she would ever wear a prayer cap on her curly hair.

Her dark winter coat will be fine, and her bag is made of leather, and hopefully will be water proof. She will have to hold her bag over her head whilst crossing the moat. The moat isn't very wide, and she has practised swimming with luggage before at home in her special swimming classes. Marieke forces her thoughts away from the moat and its content. She has to simply focus on the fjord with its blue water, and she prays fervently that her little car will be there. What will she do if it isn't? Her breath catches in her throat, the thought too awful for words. She'll have to walk along the fjord, hoping to meet a cruise ship before the Vikings catch up with her again. "When is the fight?" she asks Ingeborg, using her hands to show what she means.

"Holmgang? In morning," says Ingeborg with a little shudder. Marieke thanks her, and shudders in sympathy. Yes, she needs to get out tonight, it's her only chance. Will Sulky guard the door? "No, slepping for holmgang," Ingeborg grins when she asks the woman. Marieke is relieved that she doesn't have to worry about that, remembering the last time she tried to sneak off in the night. Together they pull the sheet off Marieke's bed, and using the dinner knife, they cut the linen sheet into long strips. Marieke ties the strips together, and at the end, they measure the make shift rope. Ingeborg looks at it, and hesitates. "Not long," she says and looks at Marieke as if she knows what to do about it. Would it be long enough? She doesn't want to land in the water with a splash, alarming the guards. They decide to cut up the bottom sheet as well. It's hard work, and it has to be done quickly as Ingeborg will need to get out, so as not to draw suspicion to themselves. Finally, it's done, and Ingeborg smiles at Marieke, showing her excitement. It is an adventure for her, but Marieke has a sick feeling in her stomach.

What if…

With Ingeborg gone, Marieke feels restless. She walks round her little room, adjusting the pitcher, straightening the sheet rope, fluffing up her pillow. Should she try to rest for a while? After all, they can't go until it's dark, and everybody is asleep. She will need her rest, as she needs to walk, then drive, if her car is there. "Lord, I need out, I need to get out tonight," she whispers, her hand touching the hot cut across her cheek, tightening with anger and revengeful wishes. Maybe she should have found something to put into the men's drinks at the table this evening. Maybe the three women should come with her, and they could put the whole castle on fire. Maybe they could poison the well or the pump or wherever they get the water from in the kitchen. Marieke spends a few vengeful minutes dreaming of sneaking into the men's rooms with her dinner knife, slashing their throats. The idea makes her feel sicker than ever; no, she could never do that to them. She can still feel her hand, wet with blood this afternoon, the rusty smell of blood enveloping her, making her head spin. She closes her eyes, her head throbbing as well now, and Marieke tries to think of the songs, beautiful hymns, filling her car, her soul…

Chapter 17

arieke wakes with a shock when shaken by Ingeborg. It is dark in her room, and very quiet. Ingeborg shushes her softly, and Marieke straightens her glasses, her hand touching her face. For a moment she feels overwhelmed, her face is scarred forever, she is still stuck inside a Viking castle, needing to escape. She takes a deep breath, trying to remember a hymn or verse, her confusion too great. She slides off the bed, pulls her boots on, grabs her coat and handbag, and walks to the door, a little unsteady after waking up so abruptly. Ingeborg has picked up the sheet rope, hiding it under her dark hooded cloak. After a last look round her room, Marieke quietly shuts the door, and taking the huge key, she locks the door, putting the key back in her handbag.

Ingeborg gives a small giggle, and then they walk quietly towards the exit door at the end of the corridor. The corridor is lit up by a single torch, which seems very bright after her dark room. Ingeborg's soft leather boots make no sound, in contrast to Marieke's boots. She tries walking on tiptoes, tries placing her feet slowly and deliberately, but the noise is still making Ingeborg throw nervous glances at Marieke's feet. In the end, Marieke gives up, pulls her boots off, and simply carries them under her arm. The tiles feel cold underneath her thin tights, but once they're out of the apartment it feels even colder. Carefully they go down the steps, staying in the shadows. The one torch lighting up the stairs, fortunately keeps part of the steps in darkness.

At the bottom of the stairs, hidden in a corner, are Gunilla and Erika, the hoods of their cloaks pulled around their faces. Gunilla's face looks flushed even in the dark, her eyes bright and excited, and after grinning at Marieke she pulls her hood tighter around herself, covering her blond hair. Marieke feels a moment of resentment. It is all very well for Gunilla to be excited; she isn't the one having to escape and walk for miles while soaking wet to avoid a forced marriage. Then she reminds herself that she ought to be grateful. Erika and Gunilla give her a brief hug, surprising her, then with a nod to Ingeborg, they slip out into the dark courtyard. The two torches near the gate light up the gate as well as part of the stairs to the battlements, casting two large circles of light. The rest is in darkness. Soon the darkness has swallowed up Gunilla and Erika. Marieke finds herself staring at where they disappeared, then Ingeborg tugs her sleeve.

She follows Ingeborg along the courtyard wall, wishing she had walked barefoot more often. No idea how she managed to walk on gritty pavements as a child! Every step hurts, and she finds herself panting and gasping with each toe stubbed, each little stone stabbing her foot. She tries to keep up with Ingeborg, fearful of losing her. Finally, they make it to the bottom of the stairs and have to cross the light circle, to get up the stairs into the darkness again. Ingeborg holds her back, peering through the darkness to the corresponding light circle on the other side.

Marieke adjusts her glasses and stares through the dark as well. They are supposed to wait for Gunilla and Erika, who will go up the opposite stairs, to attract attention, and distract the guard. That guard is in charge of the front of the castle, and Erika and Gunilla's plan to keep him to the right of the gate. Hopefully, that will allow Marieke to get up on the left, abseil down from the battlements, cross the moat, and run. In theory.

She can feel her legs beginning to shake. This was a big mistake. It will take them ages to get up to the top, tie the sheet rope onto a battlement, abseil etc, what were they thinking? She turns to Ingeborg but stops the words from leaving her mouth. What choice does she have? Staying here is not an option. Thinking of either Leer or Sulky marrying her makes her feel sick. She swallows and tries to take some deep breaths, wishing she could switch her phone on for some calm music. Ingeborg gives a sharp little gasp, and Marieke is just in time to see the split-second shadow cross on the other side. They are up the stairs! That means she and Ingeborg need to go up too. Quickly the two of them slide through the light, back into the shadows, hugging the rough stones. Marieke is shaking, her feet numb with cold and bruises. They walk up the stairs slowly, keeping their heads down. They have no idea where the guard is, and he needs to walk past the gate towards where Erika and Gunilla are.

Ingeborg sinks on her knees when they reach the top of the stairs. Marieke follows suit, giving a soft moan when she hurts her hand on the sharp edge of the step she is kneeling on. This is not her style at all, and before she realises, tears steam up her glasses. That does it, she can't be like that! She blinks wildly, willing her glasses to de-steam. Just above their heads, they can hear calm, measured footsteps, walking towards where the gate sits right underneath. The two women hug the wall, and Marieke tries to breathe quietly. The steps pass by without any change in pattern, and Marieke can feel relief growing with each step. Soon the guard's steps have gone. They wait, then suddenly hear singing, and laughing.

Erika and Gunilla! Marieke gives a very soft giggle, then quickly follows Ingeborg up the last few steps, staying low. The guard says something to Gunilla and Erika, and Marieke wished she could see what is going on. It must be working, for Ingeborg rushes to the battlement near one of the corner towers, and produces the sheet rope. Marieke swallows. What if the sheet rips with her hanging off it? What if she can't get a good grip, and she ends up with terrible rope burns all over her hands? What if… She takes a deep breath and stands close to Ingeborg who is tying the rope around a large block, willing the girl to hurry up. She gives it one last tug then turns to Marieke who has just finished putting her boots back on. She gives her a last hug, whispering, "Bee," her face rather white and ghostly in the darkness.

"Bye, and thank you very much," whispers Marieke, trying to think of more to say, simply to stretch their goodbyes, as well as delay the moment of having to step over the battlement into the dark drop below. Ingeborg puts an end to that though, as she half pushes Marieke towards the sheet rope, gently flapping in the breeze like a white lightning streak. Marieke swallows and takes a deep, shuddering breath. She climbs onto the battlement, adjusts her handbag, grabs the sheet with both hands and looks up at Ingeborg's pale face glowing right next to her. Ingeborg nods encouragingly, and whispers, "Ee run, wood," pointing to the dark shadows near the castle, which Marieke knows are the trees she needs to head for. She breathes back, "Ok, bye!" Then slowly slides off the battlement.

Seconds later she finds herself hanging well above the dark ground, and even darker water. Slowly she walks down the wall, moving her hands inch by inch. Part of her wants to hurry, needs to hurry, especially as Ingeborg hisses down, "Quick, ee quick!" Panic makes Marieke go quicker, she is sure that Ingeborg is sounding just as worried as she is feeling. Is the guard coming back or something? What if he comes back, and chops the sheet with her hanging on it? She can feel the heat on her hands and knows that she will have to be careful, otherwise she will end up with blisters all over her hands. The sheet only just about makes it to the small grass strip at the foot of the dark grey wall. Marieke sobs with relief once she reaches the ground, her arms shaking. She thought she'd have to drop down the last bit, as holding on became harder and harder. She made it though, but there is no time to revel in that. She's not out of the woods yet, or even in the woods for that matter!

Chapter 18

Marieke quickly tugs her boots off again, and one at a time, aiming for the other side of the moat, she throws as hard as she can. There is a very soft thud, but no splash, so she knows the boots made it.

Next is her coat and bag, she has to carry those whilst swimming across. She rolls her coat up tightly and puts her bag strap around it to keep it a neat package. Slowly she wades into the water. Marieke gasps, almost out loud, at the cold. Finally, she is in deep enough to swim. With quick kicks, she slowly makes her way across the moat. The opposite shore seems to drift further and further away, and she desperately keeps her eyes on the tall grass. A few times her head almost dips under the water, but kicking even faster she manages to keep her mouth dry. Her main fear is swallowing the foul water. Simply breathing in the smell makes her gag. "I…must…not…touch it!" Suddenly her stockinged toes bump the other side, and she gives a soft cry, then quickly scrambles up the grassy bank, making sure to stay low. She suddenly feels thrilled, she got out! She has escaped the castle and is on her way to freedom. She did it! She squeezes as much water out of her dress as possible, then struggles wet feet into her boots.

Marieke looks at the dark line not that far away, the tree

line. Should she commando crawl as they do in books or run as fast as possible? In the end, she decides to run, bent over. Commando crawl would take her too long. Her rolled-up coat and bag under her arm, she runs, shivering in the cold night air. Nothing can be heard, and Marieke sniffs a little when she gets to the trees. She has done it, and now all that is left is the walk to the fjord. She's shaking all over, her hands numb, her face throbbing. The small cut in her arm hurts, and her breath gives off little steam clouds. She pulls her coat back on, feeling warmer straight away, then hangs her handbag over one shoulder, pushing the large bag towards her back. She steps back towards the road a little, afraid to lose the dirt track in the darkness. There is a tiny moon, but as it's still damp and drizzly, not much can be seen. She doesn't want the guards to spot her, so she keeps to the shadows of the trees, walking as fast as she can.

How many branches can trees leave around, she grumbles to herself, after tripping up on a branch for the fifth time. She staggers a few steps, then regains her balance, but not her mood. Looking back, the castle is still very visible, a huge black block, the battlements like ugly teeth. She has been walking for ages but seems to have hardly made any progress at all. Maybe she should have organised a horse after all... Marieke turns round, determined to put some distance between her and the castle. At least the exercise makes her feel warmer, although the long wet dress clings to her legs, rubbing and hindering the taking of larger steps. She tugs at the wet dress, rearranging it so she can walk more freely. Softly humming hymns and songs, she tries to walk as fast as possible.

Marieke hears the forest noises, and they don't make her feel better at all. Are there still wolves and bears around? They used to be present during Viking times, but if this is merely a hippy commune, then they wouldn't be, of course. On the other hand, the fact that the other women had been that intrigued by her pen and paper made her wonder about the whole timing. Mind you, if those women have been living in the commune since childhood, they would be intrigued. Marieke tries to keep up a cheerful conversation with herself, ignoring the fact that her very comfy boots are starting to feel less comfortable with every step. The wet tights feel sticky and seem to rub away happily. She forces herself back to thinking, wondering. "So," she softly says out loud, simply to break the silence of the night, "So, about wild animals. Do they still have them? And is it true that they're staying away from humans as much as possible? Like wolves…" She shudders, listening for a moment to the noises around her, hearing only the snapping, cracking branches and crushed leaves under her own feet.

"How do I know what all these noises are? It's probably really interesting and educational," she continues with a very cheerful voice, like a teacher introducing algebra, knowing the students will be dragging their heels into the lessons by next week. "Maybe I could follow some wildlife course back home," she adds, then looks round. Was that too loud? What if somebody is following her, somebody nearby, listening for her voice? She has never considered it, but maybe they have sentries in the woods surrounding the castle? No, the women would have known. Would a happy, human voice attract wildlife even? Like when you're talking happily to a dog, it comes to check you out? Marieke hesitates, should she hide for a moment, just to see if somebody is following her? No, she needs to get to the fjord. Fast. In the distance, across the dirt track an owl hoots, and Marieke smiles in a patronising way, feeling a bit of an expert now she can recognise a wild animal sound. "Hunting owl, there'll be a squeak from some rabbit or mouse next," she says softly, still hating the lack of human noises. Should she risk starting up her phone, putting some music on with her headphones? She hates walking outside with headphones on, knowing it makes you more vulnerable to danger. Mind you, her greatest danger has just been left behind, and should still be asleep. She doesn't want to take the time to start her phone though, and the idea of shutting out all background noises doesn't sit well with her either.

Her feet are aching now, especially her big toes, and her heels. Would it be more comfy to take off her boots? Remembering the bruised feeling crossing the castle courtyard, she decides against it. Marieke walks on as best as she can, trying to avoid the sore spots. She stops, tries to wriggle her feet free inside her boots, the sore spots burning. She knows she has plenty of normal plasters in her bag, should she..? No time, she reminds herself, pretty sure that the sky behind her is turning lighter already. It can't be morning yet, can it? When will they discover she has gone?

She clenches her teeth together and starts walking again, limping more and more, eyes burning. In the distance, another animal makes a sound, and Marieke tries to look into the dark forest. Was it this side of the track, or across the dirt road? She straightens her shoulders and tries to think of another song to sing, finding herself resenting the men responsible for her plight more with each step. Harald, for bringing her here. Sulky... Her hand feels her face, hot from the exertion, the cut throbbing. "How am I going to explain that?" She hisses, fury towards Sulky making her eyes burn. "Everyone will be looking at the scar, making comments, asking questions." She thinks about some of the young men at church, who have been quite friendly, and secretly she had been hoping that they might become more than friends. Well, her chances there have suddenly dropped as well, plus, how is she going to explain that? "Two Vikings were fighting over me, and I ran away before they were going to settle the marriage question by duel." Yes, that sounds just great.

Chapter 19

The same animal sound breaks through her mutterings, and Marieke is sure that it sounded closer this time. What animal is it? She tries to think back through biology lessons, geography classes. What animals lived, or live in…where ever this is? Is she going with Viking countries? So northern Europe? Surely there used to be wolves and bears, but she's quite sure they must have died out. They have died out, haven't they? Or at least moved to further north than where people live. Also, wolves live in groups, and the noise she heard was definitely a single animal. Now, what else hunts at night? Do badgers make sounds? They're pretty big animals, real hunters, too. Foxes make funny doggie type noises, she knows that for one comes into her garden at night. They're very shy anyway.

Every time Marieke stops muttering to herself, or singing, or philosophising, she slows down, anger and resentment mixing with the burning pain in her feet. She blames Sulky and Leer most of all. The idiots; what were they thinking? She stomps on, breathing hard, glasses misting over now and again. Then mutters, "Just let it go, simply move on." But each painful step adds to her resentment until she says out loud, "I hate you! I hate you all! I wished I…" She stops. Wished what? She knows she meant to shout that she wished she'd killed them all, and picturing herself with the little dinner knife, chopping away at their tanned throats makes her stomach somersault, and she rushes to throw up in the bushes, the suddenness of it taking her by surprise. She breathes deep, calming breathes, her legs shaking, rummaging in her bag for a tissue. She knows that she could never have slaughtered them, not even close.

Poisoning them then? Slipping something in their drink, as you see in films? She laughs, imaging herself standing over their rolling, writhing figures, thrashing around on the ground, froth messing up their well-groomed moustaches. The nastiness of her laugh makes her face glow, and she is horrified with herself and her feelings. So much for Christians in the past, during persecution praying, "Father, forgive them," she thinks, shivering suddenly, knowing she'll keep this bit of her adventure to herself. Knowing what she thought is bad enough, sharing it with somebody makes it sound even worse as if she is some bloodthirsty monster. She isn't, at least normally she isn't. She has to admit that she gets annoyed by people, but then, some people can be very trying. She bites her lip, thinking to her barbed comments, eye-rolling and sighs when difficult clients wouldn't get off the phone. But these guys? They harmed her too, and never even felt bad about it, not one moment. She blocks out Sulky's shocked looks, and reminds herself out loud, "After all, it's not as if he apologised afterwards, or tried to make up for it!"

The self-pity grows with each step, as do the noises around her. Marieke stops talking to herself and listens more intently. What are these noises, are there more animals the closer she gets to the fjord? Maybe other tribes live here, she thinks, remembering the farms they had seen from the battlements, and the number of carts entering the castle each day. Maybe she is passing a farm, and they might have guards at night. Do farmers raid each other? Or are there robbers in this area? Marieke tries to hobble along faster, part of her wishing she had stayed in the castle after all. She swallows down the burning taste in her throat thinking about marrying Sulky or Leer. On the other hand, getting caught by robbers or farmer vigilantes doesn't sound like a wonderful outcome either. Or wolves. She is pretty sure that Viking areas had wolves, and probably still have. After all, wolves are being reintroduced in lots of countries now, even the Netherlands. Why wouldn't they have wolves in this area, it's ideal! Not for her just now though. Can wolves run fast? The way she is staggering along, even a small wolf would outrun her. Climb trees? Wolves can't climb trees. That's how people in stories always escape wolves. Apart from the chance that the wolf would wait underneath the tree, so she'd have to stay up in the tree till she got rescued. Most likely by Harald. So no climbing trees either. She could jump down from the tree on top of the wolf's head though, that should kill it, or at least stun it. Then, using her dinner knife she could finish it off.

The noise is getting closer, like an odd half howling, half barking noise. What noise do badgers make, she wonders again. Or jackals. That's it, jackals. They use to live here, didn't they? Or Wild Cats? Mind you, they should make more of a cat noise. Muttering and occasionally sobbing Marieke stumbles on, her dress nearly dried in the wind, her throat aching from her fast breathing, sobbing and constant muttering under her breath. Where is the fjord? How much further?

Marieke peers through the darkness, hoping to catch a glimpse of the shining water or some indication that she is getting closer to the fjord. She sniffs the air, smelling only damp forest. She tries to think back to the long horse ride to the castle, but it is hard to calculate how far it is when walking in the dark. She has to go carefully, as it's so dark and uneven. The animal sound comes again, louder, closer, definitely a howl. Coyote? Jackal? Wolf? Marieke's breath comes quicker, as she tries to walk faster, stumbling in the dark. There are rustling noises too, and again the howl, reverberating through her bones. Marieke trips up over a large branch, hurting her knee, a sob escaping at the same time as the gasp of relief. The branch that tackled her to the ground is rather large and feels sturdy. Whatever the animal is, this should do it. She grips the branch in both hands and walks on. She can't lose any time just waiting for the animal to appear.

The howl sounds again, deep, rumbling, then a high owooo, making her shiver. What sort of animal is it? If only she could see it, and know exactly what to do. The stick helps her to walk as well, and she wonders why she hadn't thought of a walking stick before. It steadies her, although she doesn't dare to lean on it in case it snaps in two. When she glances back, Marieke notices that the sky is getting lighter, although when she looks ahead, it's like looking into a pitch-black cave. The damp air has turned into a definite drizzle, cooling her hot face. Her hands are cold though, and she finds herself gripping the stout branch tighter. The rustling is close this time, so is the snarling howl, accompanied by snuffles. Marieke spins round, feeling panic crawl up her arms, reaching her stiff hands, making them shake uncontrollably. A large animal is just behind her, looking like a dog, its pale coloured eyes making her feel light-headed.

Is it a wolf? Or some annoying farm dog? But those light eyes…

The animal comes closer, sniffing the air, staring at her. Then it lifts its head and howls, before turning the sound into a growl, advancing stealthily. Marieke struggles to breathe for a moment, panic swirling her head, her eyes trying to focus in vain on the creature before her. Has she come this far, simply to be attacked by a flea-ridden dog? Will this animal tear her in pieces, so that when Harald and the others finally find out she'd made it out of the castle, all they will find is a few bones and her handbag? Or do wolves eat the bones as well? Maybe the animal will half bury her for another day, or maybe… The wolf howls again, and with its head low moves too close.

Chapter 20

Something snaps inside Marieke and taking a large step towards the animal she lifts the heavy branch high and whacks the wolf on the head. "Take that," she shrieks, "and that!" The next swing misses the animal, who has taken a step back and looks at her with its unnerving pale eyes. "Yes, you," she shouts, advancing towards the shocked creature. "I will teach you a lesson," hysteria filling her voice now, "for I didn't get out of a fortress, swim across disgusting water, walk through this horrible forest, simply to get away from one type of animal, to be eaten by another type of animal. So I will show you," she is crying now, her arms too tired to lift the branch high enough to get a satisfying swing, but even flicking the branch at the wolf seems to get her message across, for the animal suddenly turns tails, and slinks off into the woods.

"I haven't finished, you brute," she screams, hitting out blindly towards where the wolf disappeared. The branch hits a solid tree, and snaps in bits, one chunk hitting Marieke on her cheek. She cries out in pain, dropping the leftover part of the branch, and presses her shaking hand to her cheek. Has she gotten herself a new cut? Before she can decide, or shout more abuse after the wolf, another noise drifts over the endless woods. The sound of a horn. Three long blasts sound out, freezing Marieke to the spot, the wolf forgotten. The awful howl of the lone wolf was dreadful, but that sound was nothing compared to this one. This is the sound of human hunters, who won't be beaten off with a stick that easily. She won't be able to intimidate them, sending them packing with their tail between their legs, simply by brandishing a stick and shrieking abuse at them.

No, speed is her only option against this new danger. Marieke spins round and stumbles on as fast as she can, whimpering against the pain in her feet, her glasses steaming up. "Lord, please help, I can't do this alone," she sobs, brushing tears away angrily. "I will trust You and be kinder and more patient with people, and…and…" She tries to think fast, a voice in her head telling her that trying to make a deal with the Almighty is not really the way forward. What if God wants to teach her a lesson in trust, and acceptance, and that getting married off to some Viking is part of His plan? "No, no, it can't be, I can't be stuck in…here," she cries out loud, arguing with that awful voice in her head. Her head simply replies with a good imitation of Leer's sniggering laugh, and Marieke, blinded by tears and frantic with fear finds herself face down on the ground, all her breath knocked out of her. "Ouch, ow," she gasps, struggling back on her feet, although exhaustion makes staying down very attractive. No time to lose though, for no doubt the men will be on their horses by now, galloping down the dirt track after her.

When she looks up, she suddenly sees the fjord, the water dark, glistening in the dark grey light. "The fjord," she gasps, hope growing faster than the morning light, as she quickly dries her tears, putting her glasses back on with an impatient flick of her hand. She simply has to make it, getting caught this close to the fjord is not an option. The subtle dawn has the advantage of allowing her to see better, and Marieke throws caution to the wind and starts hobbling along the dirt track out in the open. Again she wonders if she's better off with her boots or without, but looking at the rough stones on the road, she knows that a few blisters will be better than her feet cut to shreds by the track. She is gasping for air, but determined not to slow down, her panic-stricken mind trying to work out how long it will take the castle men to get a horse, and catch up with her. Not long, that's for sure.

Suddenly the track widens out, and there is the beach, black spots indicating old fires, and thinking back to her first morning, she shivers. She looks back, sure she can hear noises coming closer. Horses? She staggers across the sand towards the ferry. Well, where the ferry was. It was here, wasn't it? This is the right beach, isn't it? She looks around, half crying now, panic rippling up her heart like the little waves before her. She keeps running on towards where the ferry used to be, looking at the foot of the cliffs surrounding the dark blue water. Where is the ferry? Marieke is sure she can hear horses in the distance, but her heart is beating so loudly, she can't tell for sure. The only certain thing is that the ferry is no longer here. Marieke's eyes fly across the dark water, looking for the large boat, but no, the ferry is no longer here. She can't see her car either, and Marieke hesitates. What should she do? She is still convinced that the fjord is her way out. Suddenly she makes up her mind. She is going down the fjord, towards where the cruise ship was seen. She will hide, and when it's proper daylight, she will make up her mind. In the meantime, she is praying for another cruise ship or a ferry. Whichever one is first.

She will need the Vikings off her trail though. Are Vikings incredible trackers? She's pretty sure they must have been experts at it in the past, but as she's still not sure how real they are, she doesn't know for certain. One thing she does know is that she can't take a chance here. She walks to the beach and stops at the water's edge. Should she take her boots off, and swim along the shoreline, or would simply wading in ankle-deep water do it? The problem is, if she gets this wrong, all her efforts will have been for nothing. Abruptly, she pulls off her boots and tries to stuff them at least partly into her bag. Next time, she is going to get herself an even larger bag. The list of 'just in case' when it comes to what one needs in a bag has just been added to. Now, what about her coat? It's not very long, but definitely over her middle, so Marieke takes if off and folds it on top of her bag.

She steps into the water, which is petrifyingly cold, her blistered feet stinging fiercely. Whimpering and sobbing, Marieke wades further into the water, hopping along on tiptoe. She follows the fjord, finding the current pushing against her. Staring through the semi-darkness, she plods on and on, her feet and legs soon numb, her teeth clattering together loudly. Every breath comes out in a low moaning sound, and Marieke feels she probably makes a pathetic picture, but she no longer cares. On and on she hops, her eyes blurry, arms shaking with the effort of keeping her bag above the water. Finally, she is past the open beach, and rocks are scattered nearer the waterline. Marieke slows down. What if there are rocks underwater as well? With her feet this numb, she could break her toes and not even realise.

She has to swim for it. That's the only option. So, treading water, she lifts her bag onto her shoulder and kicks erratically at the icy water. Something will need to be done soon, she realises that, but she has to be safe. Her arms can't cope any longer, and Marieke turns over onto her back, and sits her leather bag on her chest, and gently kicks the water. She might not be fast, but at least she is moving. She looks towards the ending of the track, now surprisingly far behind her. A chill is overtaking her whole body, and Marieke knows that she needs to get out.

Just as she comes to that conclusion, she notices the movement near the end of the track. Horses! They're here! She must get out right now. She steers towards the rocks and huddles in between some huge boulders. Staying low, she works her way past a few more, then spots a huge crack between some of them. Is it a cave? Would it be a good hiding place? If it's a place that everybody knows, they'll look here, won't they? Mind you, she has come a long way, and they might not realise that she is a good swimmer. She smiles grimly thinking of all her trophies at her parents' home. At least all those hours in the pool paid off properly! Marieke pushes her bag into the crack, then pulls herself out of the water, shaking like a drowned poodle. She wrings out her dress as much as she can, then squeezes into the dark gap.

Chapter 21

It is a cave, soft sand and larger pebbles cover the floor, but it keeps the wind and the rain out. Marieke sobs with relief, and struggles back into her coat. Trying to get her arms into the sleeves is almost impossible, and for a moment she wished she had brought her Viking cloaks. Once inside the coat, she curls into a ball in the furthest corner, praying no spiders are waiting for her there. The cave is dark, but gradually her eyes get used to it, and again she inspects the walls, but she can't see any creatures. She rocks herself, rubs her arms, swings her arms, gently thumbs her feet…anything to get warm and to get her circulation going. Daylight is crawling into the cave by now, keeping most of the cave in the shadows. Marieke crawls towards the entrance, and peeks out, but can't see or hear anything. Should she stick her head out and look? What are the Vikings up to?

She stands up, and pushes out of the opening with just her head and shoulders, only to drop back down immediately. Some men are quite close to where the rocks joined the beach, and they're looking all over the beach. There is no way they can see her, and she is a long way from those first rocks, but seeing them so close makes her breath come in panicky gasps. Do they have a boat? Will they explore the coastline by boat, and spot this cave? Marieke retreats into her corner and huddles up. She will have to wait till they're gone. She's still shivering, but feeling better than she did earlier. She's also feeling rather pleased with herself. After all, it was a long way, in crazily cold water, with her heavy bag. Maybe she should take up swimming again after this is all over. Do a lifeguard course in England or something like that. Would all her swimming diplomas transfer? It would be annoying having to redo all those exams.

The morning trudges on, and Marieke leans her head on her arms, feeling so tired. To distract herself, she digs into her huge handbag and finds some peppermints near the bottom. "Eet smakelijk," she tells herself, although it's probably the worst breakfast she has ever had. Soon after her meal of Dutch peppermint, she dozes off, too exhausted to keep her eyes open any longer. When she wakes up, it's afternoon. The shadows in the cave have swapped sides, and Marieke straightens her glasses after rubbing her eyes back to open and functioning. She carefully crawls back towards the opening, and peers out. Nothing. She stands up and slowly sticks her head and shoulders out of the gap, then freezes on the spot. There are some of the men, their yellow blond hair wafting in the breeze, near the water's edge. They are quite a long way off, but the thing that makes Marieke stare in horror is the small canoe one of them is climbing into. Slowly she lowers herself back into the cave. What is she to do? The gap is a little way above the water, but not much. Will the guy come in and look? Will he have one of those burning torches?

She withdraws as much as possible, her thoughts spinning off in every direction. They must not find her, that is the one thought Marieke can get straight. They really must not find her. She looks at her bag, her outfit, and pulls back into the darkest shadowy part of the cave. Taking a deep breath she turns her back on the opening, knowing that the white, or by now probably rather off-white Steristrips will show up, as well as the frame of her glasses. It only needs the slightest bit of light, and it will reflect off the rim or even the lenses themselves. She pulls her hood over her hair. Now all she can do is wait. Wait and pray. "What time I am afraid, I will trust in Thee," she whispers to herself, not sure that she believes that at this moment. After all, she has been so afraid these last few weeks, and nothing has gone right. What if the men find her?

They will drag her out of her cave, take her back to the castle, and she will end up marrying Leer or Sulky. She can't allow that to happen, she can't do it. What should she do if the man finds her cave, and grabs her? She has the dinner knife, but will that be enough? She pulls it out of the bag with shaking hands and looks over her shoulder. Should she attack the intruder before his eyes have a chance to adjust? Her heart drums away, all she wanted was to go home, see her parents and friends. Instead, she is stuck in a cave along a fjord, with a dinner knife in her hands, waiting to murder a Viking. What if he is stronger than her, and grabs the knife? She'd be finished, that's for sure. Tonight she'll be a Viking bride.

Marieke feels tears burning simply by thinking about it. No, she won't submit to that, she'd rather...she swallows, yes, she'd rather die. A thought comes to her mind. If she dies in this weird time warp, for that is what she is beginning to believe it is, will that bring her back to Dover? Or will she simply die, and her body will never be recovered and her family and friends never find out what happened to her? She imagines herself crouching near the entrance, waiting with the dinner knife, stabbing one Viking after another to death, pushing their bodies into the fjord, with her laughing at their gruesome end. A thought floats through her head, humming out loud in the quiet cave, "…but if you do not forgive, neither will your Father which is in heaven forgive your trespasses." Marieke draws her breath in sharply. She can't forgive, she might not be able to kill them, or even stab them, but she can't simply forgive. Does that mean she's not forgiven either?

She suddenly ducks down, further into her coat, deeper into the shadows. Something can be heard outside, and suddenly a man's voice, very loud, shouting something. Then scrabbling noises. Marieke stays still, holding her breath, sobs stuck in her throat. 'Forgive', her head nudges, 'forgive them their trespasses', but Marieke clamps her lips together, fury against the man making the knife in her hand tremble. The little bit of sunlight disappears, and with it the last bit of hope in Marieke's heart. The man is coming in. She hears a snort, then the light reappears, and the man's voice calling out again outside. Grating noises, splashing in the fjord water, then quiet. The tears drip onto Marieke's hands as she realises that the man didn't see her. She is safe! She sobs with relief, pushing the whole forgiveness issue from her head. She's safe, so she's not going to harm either them or herself, so there is no need to figure out whether she should forgive her kidnappers.

Marieke stays where she is for a very long time, just in case they check the cave again. Nothing happens though, and when the entire cave has gone dark again, Marieke crawls to the entrance to have another look. It's not completely dark outside, but close. She has a good look round, then stands up again.

She spots a group of men on the beach, one of them blows a horn, and to her enormous joy, they mount their horses and are soon trotting up the rough track, leading to the castle. They have given up the hunt! Marieke does a little dance in her cave, soon sitting down again after she knocks her head on a low point. So the men have gone. Should she try and locate her car now? Her legs feel stiff after the cold, cramped day, and when Marieke looks out of the cave, she is worried by the incoming darkness. How will she make it back to the beach? She doesn't fancy swimming again.

Far off in the forest, she hears the howl again that she heard last night. The wolf. Is he still around? Marieke stares off into the distance and then decides to wait for first light. How will she make sure to wake up in time though? Her fingers curl around her phone, should she try to set her alarm? The phone won't switch on though, not surprisingly after all that time. In the end, Marieke decides she will have to risk it. She looks around the cave and tries to make it as comfortable as possible in the area where the sunlight was this morning. Hopefully, the light on her face will wake her up.

Chapter 22

Marieke groans, and tries to roll over, the light having done its job. Everything aches, her entire body feels battered by what seemed such soft sand. It was soft, but only for a very short while, she decides, rubbing her face to try and get warm. Then she staggers towards the opening. She has to make it back to the beach, preferably via the rocks. Is that even possible? She leans out, trying to look on top of her cave. Yes, there is a way out, but will it get her all the way to the beach? Marieke pulls her bag over her head and pushes the weight towards her back.

One sharp, dark grey rock leads to another rock, and panting and sweating, Marieke makes her way towards the beach. The climb seems never-ending, but whenever she stops to have a look, she is amazed at how much nearer the beach is. Finally, her legs shaking, and with her knees imagining themselves to be double-jointed, she sinks on the soft sand. She got this far, now for her car. Marieke decides to follow the beach the other way, past more bushes and rocks. She staggers on, her feet still very sore and blistered from the long walk. Marieke is breathing hard, she didn't eat yesterday, apart from every single peppermint in her bag, some very old liquorice, and a crumbly biscuit. Even porridge sounds attractive. Almost. She walks further and further along the beach, her feet sinking in the soft sand.

Rounding a large rock covered in shrubs, she gives a sobbing shout of relief. Unbelievable. For she suddenly sees it. The red tin box, sitting on the sand. Her cry of exultation is echoed by the triumphant cry behind her. Whipping her head around she sees horses, the men leaning forward as if willing themselves closer to her, their eyes gleaming in the early morning light. The Vikings have returned to look for her! Marieke starts wailing, whimpering, sobbing, whilst pulling her dress above her knee, sprinting for all she is worth towards her red car. Her feet twist and stumble, but Marieke doesn't take her eyes of the little Fiat, and only drops her dress when she is mere steps away from her car, swinging her handbag to the front, yanking the front zip open, her frozen, shaking fingers curling round her key.

"Don't drop it," she tells herself in a desperate, terror-filled voice, "don't drop it, and don't miss." She doesn't miss, but stabs the key straight into the lock, twists, pulls the door open, and throws herself into the driver's seat, shutting the door whilst adjusting her large bag at the same time. Her long dress is caught in the door, but she doesn't care. She stabs the key into the ignition, sobbing prayers at the same time. "Please, let the car start, please let me get away, please let them not get to the car in time, oh please, oh, I can't...I can never," she cries out loud now, tears dripping onto her bag, hardly able to see anything ahead.

The car starts, it starts the first time, a small miracle in itself, as the poor tin box has sat on the beach in all weathers for quite a few weeks only slightly sheltered by the cliffs. She rams the gear stick into first gear and fights against the urge to floor the accelerator. This is the beach after all, and if she gets it wrong, she might merely dig the wheels into the sand, allowing the Vikings to catch up and simply drag her out of her car. That reminds her, and she hammers down the little pin, locking the car door. Then she's off, the car struggling against the sand, but she's moving. Looking in her rearview mirror, she screams. The Vikings are close, very close, and one of them raises a spear and throws it at the car. Marieke screams again, not just in terror, but in absolute fury as well, hurting her throat, and she yanks the car sideways. The spear misses, and she regains control of the car, swerving off the beach onto another track. Marieke prays frantically that her tyres will cope with the stones, that this track will go somewhere safe. Safer.

When she looks in her mirror again, she can see the Vikings standing on the edge of the beach, looking at her disappearing in her little red car. She recognises Harald, standing next to his horse, arms crossed. Is that Leer next to him? Sobbing quietly, relieved beyond words, Marieke blinks wildly. She has to stop crying, or she won't see a thing. Gripping the steering wheel tightly, she manages to wipe at her eyes with one hand. Suddenly, round the bend, the road smooths out. She gasps, "What, hey? That's tarmac," and staring through her windshield Marieke sees the most beautiful smooth, grey tarmac ever, her tin box purring happily. Maybe it had been a hippy commune after all then, and this is the main road to what…Oslo? Good, there should be a Dutch consul or embassy in Oslo, so she can put in a complaint against this crazed commune, and sort out her passage home.

The road twists in what is definitely a motorway slip road,

and Marieke gives a cheerful whoop, loving motorways more than ever. Then goes quiet, for the sign on the motorway says "Jabbeke 5". Jabbeke? Jabbeke as in Belgium, the motorway services at Jabbeke? Marieke gasps like a drowning guppy, trying to process this information, as well as keep her car on the road. By the time she manages to fill her lungs with enough oxygen to function, the exit for Jabbeke pops up in the distinctly lighter sunrise. She wants to get off, go into the services, have coffee, wash her hands... Then laughs out loud, "I just dreamed! It was all a dream," and shrieks with laughter, clutching the steering wheel to stay in her lane. Then catches herself in the rearview mirror, mud streaked face, dirt covering a once-white railway track of Steristrips across her cheek, a dark linen dress that she would not ever buy... Wild laughter turns into desperate whimpers, and Marieke rattles past the services at Jabbeke, not ready to be gaped at just yet.

Gripping her steering wheel tightly, Marieke judders on and on, staring ahead, desperate to get to her mum and dad, to get home. Antwerp, Breda...exits sounding more and familiar, the kilometres rattling by. Now and again, her breathing turns faster, like little sobs, but apart from that, the car is quiet. Marieke needs it quiet, no music, nothing. Just quiet. She has missed her music so much, longing for the chance to put her cd player on, but now she finds she needs the stillness. She stares at other road users, looking them up and down, each time breathing a sigh of relief when she sees normal hairstyles, normal clothes... Her head too full to try and figure it out, she banishes all things Viking, Hippy, Castle and other associated words from her mind. She simply needs to get home. That's all. Home.

It is still quite early in the morning when she parks up outside her parents' house. She looks at the clock on her dashboard then at the tall house. There is a light on in the kitchen, so her mum must be up. She groans with pain when stepping out of the car. The blisters on her feet feel awful, and her eyes sting with instant tears. She hobbles to the front door and rings the bell. Marieke pulls her shoulders back, standing straight, a smile hurting her cheek. Her mum opens the door cautiously, wondering who is ringing the doorbell at this time. Her eyes open wide when she sees Marieke. "Surprise," Marieke shouts, laughing, raising her arms to hug her mum. Her mum stares in horror, and Marieke feels her smile slipping.

"Your face? What happened? And you're covered in mud, and…" her mum's eyes travel up and down the length of Marieke taking in the dirt, the long dress, parts of it torn, and finally rest on her facial cut. "When did you do this? What happened?" Marieke tries to brighten her smile again, but it's harder work than she thought. "Come in," her mum says, pulling Marieke indoors, hugging her, but gingerly, her forehead creased with worry lines. "Come in, I'll make coffee. Do you want some beschuit?" Marieke feels like asking, "Does it look that bad?" But she manages to keep the words to herself, thinking that she might not appreciate the answer. Her mum always fed them beschuit when they were ill. Only Saturday mornings they had beschuit for breakfast, but it's not Saturday, which must mean that her mum thinks she's looking bad.

Chapter 23

The kitchen looks clean and cheerful, the smell of garlic, curry and bleach mixed with fresh coffee reminding her of home. "What happened to your face," her mum says as soon as they're sitting down at the kitchen table. "When did it happen? Why did you travel like that?" Marieke sniffs the coffee, the hot steam burning her nose, the smell comforting and invigorating.

"It happened yesterday evening," she says, the last night seemingly endless in her memory. It does feel like a dream, she thinks of the wolf, the endless walk, the fjord... Her mum gasps, "Yesterday evening? Before you went on the ferry you mean? What time was your ferry? It must have been early this morning, so why did you go on such a long journey like...like this." She waves her hand over Marieke, the bright line with its even brighter Steristrips, the torn, muddy dress, the various crisscross scratches all over Marieke's hands.

Marieke shakes her head, "No, the ferry was weeks ago," she says, but her mum cries out, cutting Marieke off straight away.

"What do you mean? The last time you rang you said you'd had a really busy day at work, where were you all that time then? Have you been staying with friends, and just pretending?" her mum is wavering between horror and outrage, then adds, "But your number! When you rang us the day before yesterday, it was your number. I saw it on our phone, it was your number. Look, I can even show you," and she starts to get up, but Marieke waves her down, her head feeling suddenly too light and too heavy at the same time. She pushes her coffee mug aside, then rests her head on her arms before she might pass out completely. Her mum pats her back, tutting and muttering. When she strokes her head, she accidentally touches the spot where Marieke bumped her head. She gasps in pain, and her mum's eyes widen even more, "You hurt your head? Maybe you have a concussion. How could you drive with a concussion? Why didn't you see a doctor? No wonder you got the days wrong. Why didn't you check? You know you should have called us!"

Marieke shakes her head, "No the concussion was more than a week ago," holding up her hand to stop her mum's next string of questions and comments. "I know, it's really, really weird. I thought it must have been a dream, but the cut is still here, and the dress and everything, so it wasn't a dream." Her mum sits down, looking at Marieke with narrowed eyes. Marieke sighs, leans back, her coffee back in its rightful place. "You see, I took the ferry as a surprise for you," she starts, then looks at her mum, "What's the date?" When her mum tells her, she closes her eyes. So all those weeks into Spring have gone, it's early in the year again, and however much she loves her two countries, neither a Dutch nor an English Spring excite her too much. "Well, in that case, in theory, I took the ferry last night, but…" The whole story comes out, sounding weirder and more random than it felt living it.

Marieke's mum stares at Marieke, completely dumbfounded,

suspicion all over her face, her eyes showing the story is being processed and picked apart. Marieke takes a deep, shuddering breath, and sips her coffee. She can't blame her mother, for even when trying to tell the story it makes no sense whatsoever. "Time travelling Vikings," her mum snorts after a while and takes a breath to say more. Then her eyes go to Marieke's Steristripped cheek, and she snaps her lips together, sipping her coffee instead.

Marieke groans, "I know, it does sound too weird for words. When I got back onto the motorway, I thought I had dreamed the whole thing. Until I looked in the mirror... Do you think the scar will be really bad?" Her hand trembles as she touches her cheek. Her mum frowns, looking at the long cut, leaning forward a little.

"It doesn't look very deep," she says in the end, "but it will definitely be a scar. Hopefully, it won't go all thick and lumpy." Marieke pulls a face, that's exactly what she is worried about.

"I hate those guys," she says vehemently, her whole face tight with fury. She has to take her hands off the coffee mug, knowing she is so angry, she will just crack the mug. She puts tight fists on her lap, but feeling the rough linen of her dress doesn't particularly help her to feel better. "I know hating isn't a good thing, but I do hate those people. It's weird because maybe they aren't even real people. I don't even know what I hate in that case." Her mum snorts with an unexpected giggle, admitting that it seems odd to hate something that doesn't exist. Coffee finished, Marieke rubs her temples. "I have a headache, and I'm exhausted. I'm going to have a shower, then sleep, then think about it." Her mum agrees that a shower might be a very good idea. A very good, hot, long, soapy shower, "With plenty of coconut oil afterwards," she adds, looking pointedly at Marieke's hands, and other parts of skin showing.

Marieke has a gloriously long, hot shower, followed by an even more wonderful long sleep. When she wakes up, her father is home. "Your mother told me all about your…adventure," he says with his rich voice. "It sounds just great," he adds, then laughs his infectious laugh, and Marieke has to smile, even though any thoughts of her ordeal make her want to cry. Her father merely glances at her scar, and after that, neither parent mentions Vikings or ferries. Marieke knew that would happen, as her parents hate confrontation, and always avoid bad memories. In fact, she is impressed that her mother hasn't said much more before Marieke had her shower, and told her father about it. At the dinner table, Marieke hesitates. Does she bring it up, and risk spoiling the best nasi goreng ever?

Near the end, she twirls her fork, takes a breath and looks at her father. He is still able to read her mind, it seems, for he holds up his hand before she can say a word. "All has been said that needs to be said," his voice is decisive. "It is in the past, and that is where it stays. Rehashing it will do no good, dwelling on it will give you worse scars than the one on your face. Forgive and forget, simply move on, don't think about it. It was very strange, we don't know what happened, how it happened, where it happened. Fortunately, you only have a scar on your face," again his eyes flicker quickly over the scar, and his face goes slightly darker. "It sounds like it could have been worse. Anyway, it is like a strange bad dream. Next time, always notify people where you are going, and make sure to stay near or with others. Living alone brings risks, we have talked about that before, especially for a girl. In these modern times, young people leave their family homes and go off by themselves, oblivious to the risks, but there it is." He shrugs, his hands spread out wide, in a hopeless gesture. Then simply carries on eating.

Marieke stares at her rice, the excellent nasi tasting dry and gritty. She knows her parents have never liked the idea of her being by herself, travelling alone. She could have guessed they'd see it as confirmation. "Why don't you find a job here? I saw a lovely apartment the other day if you still insist on living alone, but at least you'd be closer. You'd be near your friends as well, and distances are so much smaller, it saves you a lot of travelling." Her mum looks at Marieke, her large dark eyes excited about the idea of Marieke moving back to the Netherlands, her voice just a little too light and enthusiastic. Marieke stops the sigh that almost escapes. Not again. She shakes her head, trying to smile at her mother, and explains that she has her job, her friends and everything else in England. She likes it there, and this was just a one-off. Anyway, she'll not do a surprise trip again.

"Good," her father says with a large smile. And that is that. No Vikings are ever mentioned again, or lonely trips, or even moving back home. Marieke tries to think about it, but she feels only confusion. How come she spent several weeks in the Viking castle, to then end up on the Belgian motorway at more or less the time she would have past Jabbeke anyway? She misses her three friends a little, and wonders if there were any repercussions of her escape for them. What if Leer or Sulky had their Holmgang, their duel, and married Gunilla or Erika instead? She shivers. She would feel awful if that happened. But then, are they real? Was it like a spooky time gap? How does that even work? Every time she tries to think about it, she ends up with a headache. In the end, Marieke decides that maybe her parents' tactic is best. Forgive and forget. Well, forget really. Forgiving them is not an option. They left her with a long scar. To Marieke's relief, there doesn't seem to be a Keloid scar, the large growth of scar tissue that can happen. The line is lighter and does show, but her mum assures her that it will blend in over time.

Chapter 24

Marieke tries to have a wonderful time, eating all the Dutch food she has missed, meeting up with friends over coffee. She isn't sure how to explain her scar the first few times her friends ask her, and simply leaves it as an accident. The days pass by quickly, and before long Marieke is packing her little tin car. She kept the Viking dress as a souvenir, although seeing it raises her heart rate every time. "Drive safely," her father smiles, his eyes looking worried, "just don't stop for anything or anyone, get straight on the ferry, and straight off." Marieke nods, not bothering to explain that this was exactly what she had done on the way here. It's in the past, she reminds herself, hugging her mother. With a final wave, she is off. Somehow she feels relieved. Avoiding the one topic uppermost in her head was more tiring than she had expected. Soon her little tin box rattles along the Dutch motorways, into Belgium. Marieke stops at her favourite services, just at the Belgian border, buys more salty liquorice, more salty sweets, another pack of stroopwafels. Then she is on the road again, singing along with her favourite music, a stack of discs ready on the passenger seat.

Marieke passes the border guards, showing her passport, letting them look into the car. She is nervous as always, but not more so than usual. She joins the queue of cars, listening to a new cd. She smiles happily, eating another extra salty liquorice. Then her eye catches the tall, white ferry, and suddenly all the oxygen seems to have left her car. Her heart is drumming away wilder than any of her music, her hands around the steering wheel are shaking. What if... Marieke tries to swallow, her mouth dry and sticky with the sweet. Then anger. Anger and hatred against the men who took her off the ferry, and caused all the trouble and the lasting scar. They also spoilt her two weeks in the Netherlands, casting a shadow over it, making her tense, putting a barrier between her and her parents. She couldn't discuss any of the events with them, and they ended up simply making small talk. There is no way she can forget, or forgive. They weren't even sorry, so how could she forgive? Marieke realises that actually, her hatred has grown over the last two weeks. Avoiding the topic hasn't solved anything, hasn't knocked any edges off. It has simply increased her anger and hate. She breathes harder and harder, wanting to scream and shout, but doesn't want to attract the attention of the other car drivers.

Her mind is spinning. How can she ever forgive? She knows it's a good Christian thing to do, to pray for your persecutors, to forgive them. She just can't find it in herself to do so. She leans her head against the headrest and cries, feeling guilty as well as furious, letting the music wash over her. The calm voice, reading out a beautiful prayer slows her heartbeat enough to hear more than just the whooshing sounds in her ears. The words are old, yet refreshingly new as she thinks about the death of Christ, and how she is forgiven. That's different, the voice in her head argues vehemently. The sharpness of the voice helps Marieke, and wiping her eyes dry as well as her glasses, she suddenly notices lights going on in front of her. The other cars are all starting up. Straightening her glasses, she hurriedly turns the key in the ignition. Her hands are still trembling, but she is composed enough to follow the line of cars in front of her.

Switching off the engine once she is parked up, Marieke leans against the headrest for another few seconds, hating the idea of getting out of the safety of her little car. Getting out on the car deck takes self-control, and following people up the stairs makes her feel out of breath like a runner. This time, Marieke decides to stay near other people. No nap, no lying down, nothing, just hanging around where she can see the most people. She keeps checking over her shoulders, and she is aware of some of the funny looks people give her. She doesn't care. No Viking is going to surprise her twice on the same ferry. She buys a coffee, and perches on a high bar stool, constantly looking around. Marieke sips the coffee, too tense to taste it. This time she hears the request for all car passengers to return to their vehicles loud and clear. There is no way she could have missed it the first time though, and Marieke feels like going up to the information desk to ask about the first ferry. Did it ever return to Dover? Surely the cruise ship must have seen it moored in the fjord? Taking a leaf out of her parents' book, she doesn't bother asking. She doesn't want to know, it's all in the past. She repeats the lie to herself long enough until a large part of her believes it. Almost believes it, anyway.

She makes sure she is right in the middle of the crowd going down to the car deck, knowing she's being quite rude, but her one thought is to stay near others who don't resemble Vikings in any way, shape or form. She avoids anyone with blond hair, any man with long hair and anyone being loud. Sinking into the driver's seat of her car, Marieke exhales loudly. She's shattered, her whole body shaking, the back of her shirt soaking wet. Who needs a gym when simply going on a ferry leaves you feeling just as exhausted and sweaty? She clicks the key in the ignition, so her music can come back on. She drinks the last bit of the now decidedly frappe coffee in her huge travel mug, and slowly feels herself coming back to normal. Normal enough to be able to drive safely anyway. She does keep a sharp lookout though, knowing she won't feel right until she is well away from this ferry.

Marieke struggles to keep her face neutral and pleasant for the border guards lining the street. Truth is, she could have hugged them all, seeing she got off the ferry in her own car, her own time, her own world, revelling in the very English slogans and road signs. Turning up the music, singing along as loudly as she can, Marieke's mood improves with every mile. Only stopping at some services for fresh coffee and to stretch her legs, Marieke makes good time, and parking her car outside her little cottage, she sobs with relief. She made it! Her house looks the same, her garden hasn't changed, apart from flowers making it look like proper Springtime. Struggling with happy tears, she drags her suitcase into the cottage, locking the door carefully behind her. That night she sleeps without horrendous dreams for the first time since escaping the ferry Vikings.

After breakfast, she rings her best friend Lydia, and they meet up in town for coffee. Marieke smiles, the scar on her face hurting with the effort. Lydia gasps and looks at the scar in shock. "Oh Marieke, how did that happen? What did you do? That's a huge scar, will it go away eventually? Did it need stitching? Where did it happen? When did you get back?" Lydia takes a break to take another deep breath, and Marieke manages to jump in before the list of 20 questions has been asked within 20 seconds.

"I'll tell you all about it, I promise," she says, "What coffee do you want? Latte? And which cake?" Together they go up to the counter to choose cakes and order drinks. Once the two women sit down, Lydia looks expectantly at Marieke, and Marieke starts quickly, as she can see another string of questions forming in her friend's head. "It started on the ferry, on my way to see my parents," she says, taking a deep breath to calm herself down. "You see, I had taken the night ferry, and I slept. When I woke up…" The whole story comes pouring out, merely interrupted by the arrival of their coffee and cake. Marieke is grateful for the small break, but quickly carries on when she sees Lydia putting down her latte with a frown, her eyes moving side to side, questions clearly stacking up in her mind. Lydia is a very satisfying audience, gasping in the right places, tut-tutting over shocking behaviour, nodding, cringing…Marieke almost feels tempted to embellish the story.

Chapter 25

When Marieke finishes the whole story she leans back, finishing her coffee, wondering how rude it is to clean her cake plate with her finger. Lydia sighs contentedly like one would at the end of a thrilling film. "That's such an amazing story, history I mean," she adds quickly, seeing Marieke's eyes widen. "It sounds so incredible, what did your parents say?" She looks at Marieke, her blue eyes glistening. Marieke rolls her eyes and explains that after she told her mum, the subject was never brought up again. "That's hard," Lydia scrapes almost through her saucer to get the last cake crumbs off. "You see, you can't really forget, not something like that, and especially not if and when there is a physical reminder." A tiny corner of the guilt heap crumbles, leaving Marieke lighter than before. "And to forgive, well…"

Marieke nods emphatically, "I just feel so bad, but I hate those guys. I just can't forgive, especially as they never asked my forgiveness. They didn't even show the slightest signs of remorse, so surely that means I don't have to forgive? They're my enemies, so it's not about forgiving my brother seventy times seven times. I mean, I know about forgiving your enemies and all that, but I'm no longer with them, so…" She leans back, resigned to the fact her cake is as finished as it will ever get.

Lydia admits the same defeat, putting her saucer down slowly. Marieke tightens a little, she knows that look, and the fact that Lydia is quiet is not a good sign either.

"You can't forgive sins like God," Lydia starts, "It's not that kind of forgiving I suppose. It's not undoing their wrong, not even pretending they didn't do bad stuff to you. It's an attitude I believe, a readiness in your heart to realise that everything is in God's Hand. To know that they only could do to you what He would allow. To acknowledge there was an aim and a purpose in what you went through. To forgive would maybe mean to be ready to accept that we are all equal in what we could do to others." Marieke cringes, she can have the occasional grumpy day, but not anywhere on the same scale as Sulky! Of course, before the whole Viking ferry incident, she would have said the same thing. If Lydia had seen their callousness though, and their hardness, she wouldn't have said what she just said, Marieke is sure about that. Lydia must have guessed from Marieke's face that she would love to argue that point, so she rushes on, "You see, if you don't forgive them in your heart, it will eat away at you. To forgive is really to accept, and move on, having learned from it, and incorporated it into your life. It's to say that you forgive those Vikings, that you don't hold a grudge, you don't seek their destruction even if you could get back to wherever it was, and that you refuse to hate."

Marieke nods, slowly, processing her friend's words. Yes, that does make sense. On the other hand, it was a horrendous experience and has ruined travelling by herself. She has always loved going on the ferry, now it has turned into the most stressful thing ever. Simply because of those Vikings, who don't even care. Or didn't anyway. "I hate what they have done to my life. I know I can't get to them, so I can't do anything to them. But I dream about it, and every time I think about them I feel so angry." Lydia nods and explains that to forgive has never been an easy thing. She points out that it's always been connected to our forgiveness in Christ. Marieke feels her face warming up. It reminds her of the cd she was listening to whilst waiting for the ferry. "It reminded me, and it did put things into perspective," she admits. Lydia smiles, opens her mouth to say something, then closes it, sipping her latte instead. Marieke is grateful and smiles at her friend.

Marieke gets up to order another coffee, she just needs the break, needs the headspace. Back with her hot coffee, she stirs it endlessly. "I like the moving on idea. I must admit, I felt like I was still stuck in the whole experience, you know, hating them, wanting to harm then, thinking of ways to avenge myself. I don't even know how to get to them! Are they in our time? It was the weirdest thing, and I think it's the not knowing that's been the most difficult. I like the moving on, you know, the not even worrying whether it was in the here and now, but to simply forgive in my heart, and live with the lessons. I'm just not sure that I can. I would love to see them punished, and for them to suffer for the awful time I had." She touches her cheek, her eyes burning.

Lydia looks out of the window, "It might be a process, you know, first the willingness, then the saying the words out loud. A bit like the 'fake it till you make it' type thing." Marieke agrees, yes, she can see herself doing that. Her thoughts drift to her parents and their attitude. Simply pretending it never happened, merely move on with life. No wonder so many friends of her parents have health issues. "Yes, you can't just move on, wishing the memory doesn't exist, pretending all is well. Your body will respond physically, to make you stop and think." Marieke sighs, knowing the truth of that statement. She has had constant headaches, her heartrate spiking every time she thought about Vikings, ferries or castles.

"It's like letting them off lightly though. After all, their lives just carried on, and I have the nightmares, the scar, and the fears. Nothing will ever be the same again." Well, that might be a bit dramatic, after all, she is having coffee as usual with a friend. Marieke takes a deep breath, "I know I should forgive them, as I'm forgiven. But surely there is a difference between me rolling my eyes at an annoying client, or wishing they'd get the message and get off the phone or kidnapping a person, hurting them, and scarring them?" Lydia nods, her face paler than usual, her eyes wide simply thinking about the horrors Marieke had been through.

"It sounds just so awful," she says, her face empathetic, "but do two wrongs make a right? You see, if you only think of revenge, or getting them to suffer, aren't you the one hurting the most? It's like taking poison, hoping the other person will die from it…" Marieke smiles at that, yes, she's heard that before. "It's going to be hard," Lydia says, her voice soft, and Marieke nods, tears misting up her glasses. "You see, doing the right thing is never easy or straight forward, but it's still the right thing. It's counting your blessings." Marieke sighs at that and tells Lydia how she struggled with that whilst stuck in the castle. "There, see!" Lydia smiles, "And what blessings did you find that day?" Marieke's eyes go dreamy as she thinks back to the better times. Lydia is right, she needs to find a way to let go, to move on.

She feels relieved as well, as if the cloud has been dispersed, and the sun has finally broken through. The rest of the morning is spent talking about Gunilla, Erika, Ingeborg, healthy but bland food, the beauty of the sunny fjord. Talking about it with Lydia helps to pick out the good bits, the parts that were a blessing after all.

Chapter 26

Walking back into her cottage, Marieke touches her face. Her sunny mood is clouded over when she feels the rough scar. It is easy for Lydia to tell her what to believe or accept, but there should be a restoration of some kind. Marieke is sure that by simply forgiving the Vikings, she is denying the terror she felt all those weeks. She pours herself a coffee, her mind faster than her hands. "There was no restoration, no repentance. It might not have been awful all the time, but I was a slave girl." The whispered word, trälinna, stuck in her head. There is no way she will ever forget that word or the looks the other women threw her when they mentioned the word.

Marieke sips the hot coffee, its warmth reaching her heart. She mulls over the words Lydia spoke and pulls a face. She has to agree with the words, but her heart doesn't agree with her head on this one.

It is not till a few days later when Marieke is making herself a sandwich. Her radio plays in the background, beautiful music filling her sunny room. Marieke is smiling, looking forward to lunch after a busy morning. The music is replaced by the interviewer's voice, and Marieke sighs. Some of the interviews are interesting, but she prefers soothing music. She tunes out, sprinkling curry powder on her cheese sandwiches, until she hears the voice, "…interesting to hear about the cruelty of Vikings, after all the positive stories that are around." The buttered knife clatters onto the worktop. Marieke can't breathe, her knees shaking. Another voice answers with an apologetic laugh as if the person feels for people having their ideal Viking image shattered. The words swirl around Marieke as she stands at the worktop, her hands clamped around the edge to steady herself. When the music returns, some strength returns with it, and she manages to take her plate to the sunny dining table. Chewing carefully, she thinks about what she has heard.

One thought remains with her. Despite Sulky and Leer, nothing really dreadful happened to her. Her fingers trace the scar, smoother now, and she blinks back tears. Yes, she had been terrified. Yes, she still doesn't know how or what happened to her, but none of it was as horrifying as the woman on the radio had shared. Nobody harmed her, at least not on purpose. They fed her, clothed her, and allowed her to wander around the castle. Sulky pushed her over, hurt her when she tried to escape, but he didn't harm her. She swallows. Trying to escape could have resulted in dreadful punishment if the radio interview was to be believed. She blinks back new tears. "Thank You, Lord, for protecting me."

She traces the sunny outline on the white table and finds the hatred has gone. It's a lot easier to think of the beauty and kindness she has encountered in the last few weeks of her involuntary stay. Ferry crossings will never be the same again, and that does make her sad, feeling the loss. But before her mind can compose a list with other things that will never be the same again, Marieke casts her mind back to the beauty of the views across the fjord, saying out loud, "Plus I will never take herbs and spices for granted again. Or coffee," taking her plate into the music-filled kitchen with a grin.

Acknowledgement

I hope you have enjoyed this Novella. I was thrilled to find there were such things to be found, for I wanted to enjoy some Viking story, but not a full novel, so here we are! I love Living Vicariously, and this presented itself with the perfect opportunity. I love travelling to the Netherlands to see my parents, friends and family. I also enjoy reading about Vikings, so, through Marieke, I spend a wonderful living vicariously!

I have mixed some of the Viking Era together. For example, glass was used later on, as were Viking castles. I wanted a castle, inspired by my childhood favourite book, Erik De Noorman, so I was relieved when I found out that there were castles, how ever few.

Thank you, Beverley Haagensen, for once more editing my ramblings, and making the book a lot better than it would have been otherwise.

I'm grateful to Richard, my husband, for supporting me, and allowing me space and time to write.

And I'm grateful to my Lord and Saviour, for forgiving me and blessing me with so many blessings, that to count them all would be a fulltime job. I enjoyed this opportunity to think more about forgiveness and repentance.

As always, I love hearing from you, so do visit my website,

https://vicarioushome.com and sign up for my mailing list to stay in touch! Or find me on Instagram and Facebook, under @Vicarioush.ome.

Do check out my other books, Sapphire Beach, Walled City and later in 2021, Beyond The Hills.